PUFFIN BOOKS

The Unluckiest B...

Andrew Norriss was ... ...land in 1947, went to university in Ir... and taught history in a sixth-form college in England for ten years before becoming a full-time writer. In the course of twenty years, he has written and co-written some hundred and fifty episodes of situation comedies and children's drama for television, and has written four books for children, including *Aquila*, which won the Whitbread Children's Book of the Year in 1997.

He lives very contentedly with his wife and two children in a village in Hampshire, where he acts in the local dramatic society (average age sixty-two), sings in the church choir (average age seventy-two) and for real excitement travels to the cinema in Basingstoke.

Books by Andrew Norriss

AQUILA
BERNARD'S WATCH
MATT'S MILLION
THE TOUCHSTONE
THE UNLUCKIEST BOY IN THE WORLD

ANDREW NORRISS

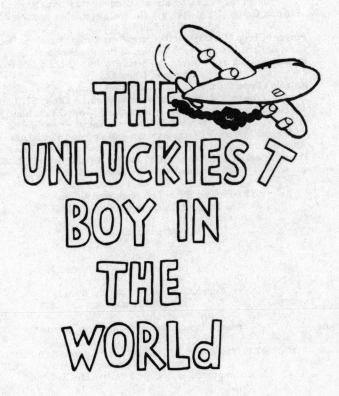

THE UNLUCKIEST BOY IN THE WORLD

PUFFIN

PUFFIN BOOKS

Published by the Penguin Group
Penguin Books Ltd, 80 Strand, London WC2R ORL, England
Penguin Group (USA) Inc., 375 Hudson Street, New York, New York
10014, USA
Penguin Group (Canada), 90 Eglinton Avenue East, Suite 700, Toronto,
Ontario, Canada M4P 2Y3 (a division of Pearson Penguin Canada Inc.)
Penguin Ireland, 25 St Stephen's Green, Dublin 2, Ireland (a division of
Penguin Books Ltd)
Penguin Group (Australia), 250 Camberwell Road, Camberwell, Victoria
3124, Australia (a division of Pearson Australia Group Pty Ltd)
Penguin Books India Pvt Ltd, 11 Community Centre, Panchsheel Park,
New Delhi – 110 017, India
Penguin Group (NZ), cnr Airborne and Rosedale Roads, Albany,
Auckland 1310, New Zealand (a division of Pearson New Zealand Ltd)
Penguin Books (South Africa) (Pty) Ltd, 24 Sturdee Avenue, Rosebank,
Johannesburg 2196, South Africa

Penguin Books Ltd, Registered Offices:
80 Strand, London WC2R ORL, England

www.penguin.com

First published 2006

8

Copyright © Andrew Norriss, 2006
All rights reserved

Set in Monotype Plantin by Palimpsest Book Production Limited,
Polmont, Stirlingshire
Made and printed in England by Clays Ltd, St Ives plc

British Library Cataloguing in Publication Data
A CIP catalogue record for this book is available from the British Library

ISBN-13: 978-0-14-131877-6

www.greenpenguin.co.uk

Mixed Sources
Product group from well-managed
forests and other controlled sources
www.fsc.org Cert no. SA-COC-1592
© 1996 Forest Stewardship Council

Penguin Books is committed to a sustainable future
for our business, our readers and our planet.
The book in your hands is made from paper
certified by the Forest Stewardship Council.

CHAPTER ONE

Until he was eleven years old, Nicholas Frith never thought of himself as particularly lucky or unlucky. Some good things had happened to him, like getting his own computer, and some bad ones, like never seeing his father, but nothing really exceptional one way or the other.

When he was eleven, however, he was very unlucky. On holiday in Spain, he disturbed the grave of Toribio de Cobrales – a man who had been dead for nearly three hundred years – and fell under a terrible curse. Nicholas had never meant to disturb a grave, least of all one with a curse on it, but unfortunately that's what he did, and this story is what happened to him as a result.

He and his mother were staying in an apartment

at Albunol, a small town to the east of Malaga, and on the fourth day of their holiday Mrs Frith hired a taxi to take them on a trip into the mountains. Driving north, towards the snow-covered peaks of the Sierra Nevada, they drove along roads cut into the side of steeply hanging gorges, and through little villages of white painted houses.

Their driver, Miguel, pointed out the sights and explained the history of the places they passed. He spoke in Spanish, so neither Nicholas nor his mother could understand what he was saying, but it didn't seem to matter. Every so often, Mrs Frith would tap him on the shoulder, use her hands to explain that they wanted to stop and he would pull over so they could get out and admire the scenery.

Towards the end of the day, they had stopped to stretch their legs one last time and were heading back to the car, when Nicholas announced that he needed to go to the toilet.

'I'll catch you up,' he told his mother. At eleven years old, he liked a little privacy for these things and made his way behind a large rock, stuck upright in the ground. Unzipping the front of his trousers, he noticed that the side of the rock that shielded him from the road was covered in writing.

He could not read any of the words – they were all in Spanish – but he liked the pattern they made as they spiralled round in decreasing circles towards a small nine-pointed star in the centre of the stone. He was wondering, idly, what they might mean when he glanced down and realized that, instead of the water landing on the ground, it was disappearing into a hole at the base of the rock.

A moment later, as he was zipping up his trousers and about to walk back to the car, he heard a shout.

'*Aiee!*' Miguel was standing by the taxi, furiously waving his hands. '*Alejate! Alejate!*'

He ran up the hill towards Nicholas, grabbed him by the arm and was anxiously pulling him back towards the car, when he glanced at the place behind the stone and froze. He was staring at the hole in the ground and the wet marks splattered around it.

'*Madre de Dios!*' he muttered, crossing himself. '*Qué has hecho?*'

Letting go of Nicholas, he knelt down, peered cautiously into the hole and stepped back almost immediately with a little gasp. '*Demonio!*' He stared in horror at Nicholas. '*Has profanado la sepultura de Toribio!*'

Mrs Frith had come to join them. 'Nicholas?'

she said sharply. 'What's happened? What have you done?'

'I haven't done anything,' said Nicholas. 'I was just having a wee.'

The taxi driver pointed urgently to the hole in the ground. '*La sepultura de Toribio*,' he whispered, hoarsely, '*La sepultura de Toribio!*'

Mrs Frith stepped forward, peered cautiously into the hole and went rather pale.

'Oh, goodness . . .' She looked accusingly at Nicholas. 'Did you have to do it here?'

'Why? What's wrong with here?'

'It's a grave!' hissed Mrs Frith.

Nicholas stepped forward and peered into the hole. It was a moment before his eyes adjusted to the gloom but, when they did, he realized he was staring into a face. It was a face that had been dead a long time but in the dry air of the mountains it had been wonderfully preserved. The skin was a deep mahogany colour and, though the eye sockets had fallen in and the skin round the mouth had shrunk to reveal the teeth, you could see it had once belonged to a strong and powerful man. There was a full head of hair on the top of his head and a long beard growing from his chin, and there was also, Nicholas noticed, a yellow liquid dripping gently from the end of his nose, down into his open mouth.

'I am so sorry.' Mrs Frith had turned to Miguel. 'He didn't mean any harm. He just . . . he didn't realize it was there, you see, and . . .'

But the taxi driver was not listening. He was running down the hill as fast as his legs could carry him. '*Espera aquí!*' he shouted over his shoulder. '*Espera aquí!*' Then, flinging himself into the taxi, he started the engine before he had even closed the door and, in a squeal of tyres on gravel, spun the car back the way they had come and drove off down the road.

It all happened very quickly and Nicholas and his mother now found themselves alone on the mountainside in a silence broken only by the sound of a nearby waterfall.

'I upset him, didn't I,' said Nicholas.

'Yes,' said his mother, 'I think you did.'

They sat by the side of the road, wondering what they should do. There were, Mrs Frith concluded, only two things they *could* do. They could sit and wait until someone came along who might help, or they could start walking back to the nearest village. Neither choice was particularly appealing.

If they waited, there was no guarantee that anyone would come, or that they would be willing to stop and help if they did. It was an isolated road and Mrs Frith could not remember seeing a car or even passing one in the last hour. On the other hand, she had no idea which direction the nearest village was, or how long it would take to walk there.

The more she thought about it, the more worried she became. She had no idea where they were, and in an hour or so it would be getting dark. They had no food, no water, no coats to protect them from the cold night air and there was . . . something else.

Across the valley, dark clouds were gathering in what had, only moments before, been a clear blue sky. The mountainside, which had seemed so sunny and open when they got out of the taxi, had become vaguely sinister and threatening. There was a sense of menace and danger in the air that she could not explain but gave her the strongest feeling that staying where they were was not a good idea.

'Come on.' She stood up. 'Let's start walking.'

Nicholas obligingly pushed himself to his feet, but sat down again almost immediately as the ground shook beneath him, throwing him off balance. It was a small earth tremor, of a kind frequent in the mountains and strong enough to send some stones skittering down the mountain-side to the road. Looking up, Mrs Frith was in time to see a rock the size of a man's fist bouncing down the hill towards them. It landed on a nearby boulder, spun off at an angle and hit Nicholas on the side of the head. His eyes closed and he fell sideways to the ground.

'Nicholas! Nicholas, are you all right?' Mrs Frith knelt on the ground beside her son and pulled his face towards her. As she did so, she saw the little patch of grass beneath his head was black and withered, as if it had been sprayed with some powerful chemical. It was the same under his hands and his legs. Wherever his skin had touched the ground, anything green beneath it had withered and died.

Mrs Frith gave a little scream, then scooped up her son in her arms and began running down the road. She had no idea what was happening or why, but she was suddenly certain of one thing: they had to get away. She was not a large woman and it was doubtful how far she could have carried an eleven-year-old boy not much smaller than herself, but she had barely reached the first bend in the road when a car came racing up the hill towards her. It was Miguel in the taxi. He screeched to a halt in front of her and a young man climbed out of the passenger seat. He ran straight over to Nicholas, looked briefly at the wound on his head, then lifted up his eyelids to look at his eyes.

'It was a rock!' There were tears welling up in

Mrs Frith's eyes. 'It came down the mountain and hit him on the head.'

The young man nodded, but showed no surprise. His eyes were anxiously scanning the hillside as if he expected some hidden danger to leap out.

'All right. I will take him now.'

He took Nicholas in his arms and carried him, briskly, back to the car. Miguel appeared the other side of Mrs Frith, tugging at her sleeve.

'Come!' There was a fierce urgency in his voice. 'Come, quick!'

He pulled her towards the car, where the young man was already laying Nicholas on to the back seat.

'Is he going to be all right?' she asked. 'Are you a doctor?'

'There is no time for questions.' The young man was climbing in beside her son. 'Please. Get in the car.'

Mrs Frith got into the passenger seat as Miguel put the car into gear and spun them round in the road.

They were only just in time. The first bolt of lightning struck as they sped off down the road, splitting the trunk of a tree not three feet from the astonished Mrs Frith.

★

Nicholas remembers nothing about that journey, but his mother remembers every second. In a matter of minutes it was dark enough for Miguel to need headlights. And then the rain came. A driving rain that pounded on the roof and sides of the car, making it impossible to speak without shouting.

Above and around them the thunder boiled and detonated with an unspeakable ferocity and, all the time, Mrs Frith continued to be aware of that indefinable sense of menace, a feeling that they were somehow under attack. It was as if the heavens themselves were trying to reach into the car and grab them all and throw them down the mountainside.

The lightning struck again and again. It hit trees on either side of the road as they passed, it split boulders, and twice it actually hit the car itself, though with rubber tyres they were shielded from its effects.

She had no idea where they were going. She tried to ask the young man cradling Nicholas's body on the back seat, but he did not answer. His eyes were closed, he was holding his hands above Nicholas's chest and from his half-opened mouth came a deep humming noise, whose vibrations filled the car. She called to get his attention but Miguel reached up a hand to stop her.

'No talk,' he said, then jerked a thumb to indicate the man in the back. 'He busy. He . . . he protect us.'

As they drove on, the storm around them became even wilder. The rain turned to hail. The thunder crashes were so loud Mrs Frith could feel the shock waves in her ears, and the whole world seemed maliciously bent on preventing them ever leaving the mountain. At one point the road was blocked by a fallen tree, which Miguel pushed out of the way with the nose of the car. A few hundred yards later rocks and earth bounced off the roof of the car as he drove through a landslide and, half a mile after that, there was a bull. An enormous animal with huge horns, facing them in the middle of the road, bellowing angrily and pawing at the surface with one of its hooves.

Miguel stopped the car and turned to the man in the back as if to ask what to do. The man stopped humming, opened his eyes and looked ahead at the bull. He made a strange sign in the air with a hand, spoke harshly in a language Mrs Frith did not recognize, and the bull, looking slightly confused, turned to one side and ambled out of the way.

Ten minutes later, they were driving through a grove of olive trees towards a large, stone farmhouse with a tiled roof. By the front door an old woman with a lantern was waiting for them. She did not speak as the car drew up, but merely turned and went back into the house as the young man carried Nicholas inside.

Mrs Frith followed Miguel into a room where the man was already placing her son on a large wooden table. The old woman took no notice of her but reached forward and tore open Nicholas's shirt. She was making the same humming noises that the young man had made in the car as she stroked his forehead and then, dipping her fingers in a bowl of mud-coloured liquid, started drawing marks on his chest.

'What is happening?' asked Mrs Frith. 'Who is she? What's she doing?'

'She is a *bruja*,' the young man replied in a low voice. 'An . . . enchantress.'

'She's a *what*?' As Mrs Frith ran forward to protect her son, the man caught her arm and gently pulled her back.

'Believe me,' he said softly, 'at the moment, she is the only one who can save your son's life.'

CHAPTER TWO

When Nicholas awoke the next morning, he was lying in a strange bed, staring up at a polished wooden ceiling, with no idea where he was or what had happened.

'How are you feeling?' His mother was sitting to one side, looking rather pale and anxious.

Nicholas thought about it and decided that, apart from a slight headache, he did not feel too bad.

'I'm OK,' he said. 'Where are we?'

'You are in my house.'

Turning his head, Nicholas saw the speaker was a young man standing the other side of the bed.

'This is Señor Herez,' Nicholas's mother explained. 'Miguel went to get him after . . . after your accident.'

'Accident?' Nicholas frowned. 'What accident?'

'You disturbed the grave of Toribio de Cobrales.' It was Señor Herez speaking again. 'In consequence, you had fallen under his curse and were in grave danger.'

'Señor Herez knows a lot about curses and magic.' Mrs Frith made a brave attempt at a smile and patted her son's arm. 'That's why Miguel went off to find him. He thought he might know how to protect you.'

'A curse?' said Nicholas. 'I'd fallen under a curse?'

Señor Herez nodded gravely.

Nicholas stared at him for a moment, then looked across at his mother.

'This is a joke, right?'

Mrs Frith did not answer.

'I wish with all my heart that it were only a joke.' Señor Herez gave a long sigh. 'If you feel well enough, I suggest that you dress and, over breakfast, I shall tell you the whole story. There is much you need to know.'

'But you don't have to worry.' Mrs Frith was patting his arm again, still wearing that bright, encouraging smile. 'Because there's nothing to worry about. Nothing! Nothing at all!'

And there was something in her voice that told Nicholas he should be very worried indeed.

*

Nicholas's breakfast that morning consisted of pieces of fruit in a bowl of yoghurt, and some bread with slices of cold meat. He ate it on the terrace at the back of the house, looking out over a valley that was dotted with fields and orchards, with the mountains rising behind them.

The air was clean and fresh, the sun was shining and Miguel had brought out a glass of orange juice for him. While he was eating, Señor Herez, sitting in a large high-backed chair of carved wood at one end of the table, did his best to explain what had happened.

'Three hundred years ago, this whole province,' he said, gesturing to the land in front of them, 'belonged to Don Frederico de la Cagalla, a most powerful nobleman. He was a grandee, a Comanderia of the Order of Alcantara, and in all this province his word was law and none dared defy him. Except one man.

'In a village in the mountains, there lived a *hechicero*, a sorcerer, called Toribio de Cobrales. He was known to have great powers and all the people came to him for healing, to settle their disputes, to bless their children . . .

'Don Frederico did not approve of sorcerers. He did not approve of men who gave out justice and blessings and magic spells. He vowed to banish Toribio from his lands and, for many years, that was what he tried to do.

'He failed. The men he sent to arrest Toribio or to kill him came back empty- handed, and Don Frederico's anger grew. He swore by all the saints that he would drive Toribio from the land, dead or alive, and personally led an army of a thousand men against him. But he was too late. Toribio had died three weeks before. To fulfil his vow, Don Frederico said he would find the grave, remove the body and throw it into the sea, but Toribio defeated him even in this. His grave was protected by a curse and no one, not even the great grandee himself, dared touch it.'

Nicholas felt a chilly sense of foreboding.

'What . . . what did the curse say?'

In answer, Señor Herez picked up a book, opened it at a page he had already marked and passed it to Nicholas. The page was covered in a writing that he recognized. The words were written in a circle that spiralled inwards towards a nine-pointed star, and the last time he had seen them was on the face of the stone on the mountain.

'In your language,' Señor Herez said, leaning across and tracing over the letters with his finger, 'it says:

"'This is the curse of Toribio de Cobrales. If any man disturb my resting place, may all manner of misfortune and calamity befall him. May anger and envy be attracted to his person. May the animals of the field and the birds of the air be his enemy. May the plants and fruits of the earth be blighted beneath his fingers. May he fail in any test or trial. And may his days be short and his existence miserable beyond hope.'"

There was silence for a moment when he had finished.

'It is,' he added, a little unnecessarily, 'a very bad curse.'

Nicholas could only agree. It sounded about as bad as it could be.

May all manner of misfortune and calamity befall him . . . May anger and envy be attracted to his person . . .

'Are you sure there hasn't been some mistake?' he said. 'I mean, curses don't really happen . . . do they?'

The words that Señor Herez had read were still ringing through his brain.

May the animals of the field and the birds of the air be his enemies. May the plants and fruits of the earth be blighted beneath his fingers . . .

Señor Herez reached across to a vase of flowers

in the centre of the table and took out one of the blooms.

'Here.' He held it out. 'Take it.'

Nicholas took the bloom and, as his fingers touched the stem, it drooped and withered in his hand.

'Don't worry.' Mrs Frith took the blackened flower and placed it on the table. 'It's going to be all right. Really it is.'

May he fail in any test or trial. And may his days be short and his existence miserable beyond hope . . .

It didn't sound like it was going to be all right.

'I didn't mean to disturb anyone's grave.' Nicholas turned to Señor Herez. 'I just wanted to go to the toilet.'

'I understand it was an accident but, sadly, that is of no account.' Señor Herez closed the book and his dark eyes looked sympathetically at Nicholas. 'We have many earth tremors in this region. Unfortunately, one of them opened the ground above the grave shortly before you arrived and you . . .'

He stopped as a tiny, very old lady appeared on the terrace and walked slowly over to Nicholas. She placed a hand on his shoulder and murmured something into his ear. It was in Spanish and, although he did not understand it, for some reason it calmed him and he felt less anxious.

'This is the Donna Alena, my grandmother,' said Señor Herez as the old woman came over to Mrs Frith and took her hand. 'She is a *bruja*. I know a little magic but I could not save you from a curse of such power. She is the one who saved your life.'

'What did she do?'

'My grandmother was able to weave a spell of protection round you last night.' Señor Herez was pulling out a chair for the old lady to sit down. 'She could not lift the curse itself – that was beyond even her strength – but she was able to weave a shield round you, a wall of magic, so that no evil may befall you.'

'You mean . . .' Nicholas wasn't quite sure he understood. 'You mean I can't be hurt?'

Señor Herez nodded. 'Nothing resulting from the curse of Toribio can harm you,' he said.

Nicholas felt a wave of relief. 'So everything's all right, then?'

'You will be safe,' Señor Herez replied carefully, 'but the curse will still operate. Misfortune and calamity will follow wherever you go. Anger and envy will dog your path. You will face the enmity of birds and animals and all these things will be drawn towards you as the moth is to the flame. You will not be harmed by them yourself. My grandmother's protection will see to that, but for those around you . . . life will not be easy.'

Nicholas thought about it, and the more he thought, the less he liked it. His mother was one of the people around him. So were his friends at home and at school . . .

'You mean, wherever I go, bad things will happen to the people around me? All the time?'

Señor Herez nodded.

'But isn't there something you can do about it?' pleaded Nicholas. 'Isn't there some way you can get rid of the curse altogether?'

Señor Herez gave a little shrug and it was Donna Alena who answered. She spoke in Spanish, and her grandson translated her words into English.

'My grandmother says that she is very sorry, but no, there is nothing else she can do.'

Later that morning, Nicholas and Mrs Frith returned to Albunol. They said goodbye to Señor Herez and his grandmother, thanked them again for all they had done, and climbed into Miguel's taxi.

The accidents began almost as soon as they left the farmhouse. They were not as dramatic as the terrible journey of the night before, but they were very persistent. First, Miguel had to stop to deal with a flat tyre. Soon after that, they were delayed by a herd of sheep that gathered round the car, refusing to move and butting aggressively at the doors. Outside Albunol, they were held up for three hours in a traffic jam caused by a woman giving birth to twins in a minibus and, when they finally arrived at their apartment, they found it had no electricity because a tree had fallen on the power line.

Next day, when Nicholas got up, he found the swimming pool had been closed because rats had been found in the filtering equipment. His mother suggested they take a trip into Malaga and the coach broke down on the motorway. The restaurant at which they tried to have lunch had to close when the chef was badly mauled by an octopus he was taking out of the fish tank. No one even suspected that any of these things were Nicholas's fault, but there was no doubt in his mind that, somehow, he was causing them.

Mrs Frith hoped that things would improve once they were back in England. She had the idea that being further away from Toribio's grave might somehow weaken the curse – but it made no difference. After a nightmare flight to Gatwick, during which the pilot had to deal with seven separate mechanical failures, they got home to find the trail of disasters following in Nicholas's path was as persistent as ever.

When he returned to school a week later, they

got worse. This was the year he was starting at secondary school and, on the first day, his classroom was burnt to the ground in a fire caused by an electrical fault. Major accidents like these did not happen every day of course, but minor ones did, and they were almost as bad. The little cuts and bruises, the slips and falls, and the angry arguments that would flare up from nowhere whenever he was around, all made life very difficult.

Mrs Frith tried everything she knew to find some way the curse could be lifted. She spent long hours reading up the subject in books she got from the library, and writing letters to people she thought might be able to help, but to no effect.

She and Nicholas both got very excited when they found an English witch who advertised on the Internet that she could provide protection from bad spells. Mrs Arcante drove down from the north of England to meet them, but a runaway cement lorry drove over her car two minutes after she arrived, and then a lump of ice fell out of the sky on to her head, on the way up to the front door. She phoned from the hospital to say she would not be coming back.

They tried very hard to keep the curse a secret, at least from all the people they met and knew locally, in case it drove them away, but it made no difference. Somehow people knew. Some part of them soon recognized that being around Nicholas Frith meant bad things happened to you. That hanging around with him was when people got their fingers trapped in doors, or slipped at the top of the stairs, or dropped scalding mugs of tea down the front of their trousers.

Even the best of friends can become nervous if such experiences are repeated often enough and, around Nicholas, they were repeated all the time. Without a word being spoken, he found he was increasingly left on his own. Few people wanted to be with him and those who did usually came to regret it.

At Christmas, his mother moved him to another school, hoping that a new start with different friends might make things easier – but the same thing happened all over again. After six weeks, the headmaster of the new school asked him to leave. He said he was very sorry, and that he had nothing against Nicholas personally but, for the sake of the other pupils, he had no choice. He and his staff were adamant. Either Nicholas left, or they would all resign.

Mrs Frith gave up her job so that she could teach Nicholas at home. She found that if he stayed indoors and went out as little as possible, the accidents were reduced in number to something that was almost manageable. So Nicholas's life was limited to the house and his garden. Occasionally, he might go out to the park or the corner shop, but whole weeks could go by without his speaking a word to anyone apart from his mother, and for a boy who had enjoyed his life and his friends, it was very hard. He read a lot of books, he watched a lot of television, he kicked a ball up and down the garden till he had worn a groove in the lawn, and sometimes he found himself thinking it might have been better if the Donna Alena had not woven her protective spell and some accident had finished the whole business at the start.

It went on like this for eighteen months, and both Nicholas and his mother had almost come to believe that it would go on like this forever.

CHAPTER THREE

The headmaster of Dent Valley School was a small, wiry man with receding hair and a bristly, ginger moustache. Despite his height – he was a good deal shorter than most of his pupils – Mr Fender was a man of some authority who had been known to reduce men twice his size to tears merely by staring at them through the lenses of his steel-rimmed spectacles.

At the moment, however, the eyes beamed benignly across his desk at Nicholas, sitting the other side.

'I see from your file,' he said, 'that you spent a term at St John's.'

'Yes,' said Nicholas.

'Then half a term at King Edward's and, for

24

the last eleven months, you've been taught at home by your mother . . .'

'Yes,' said Nicholas.

'I think it might be a good idea to make a decision about how you want to be educated,' Mr Fender said, looking down his nose, 'and then stick to it. How long are you planning to stay here?'

'As long as possible,' said Nicholas, and he meant it. It had taken many hours of argument to persuade his mother to let him try going back to school and she had told him that if it didn't work this time, they would be moving to the Outer Hebrides. They would live out the rest of their lives as far away as possible from any other human life form.

'Hmm.' Mr Fender sniffed. 'Well, you won't find it easy, joining a new school two weeks into the term. Most of the other children have already made friends and settled into their groups . . .' He stood up. 'Though I've got someone who might help you with that.'

He walked to the door and pulled it open.

'Come in, Fiona.'

The girl who came in had a slightly odd appearance. She was about the same age as Nicholas, but none of her clothes seemed to fit properly. Her blazer was too small, her skirt was too long, and her blouse too tight round the collar. There was something odd about her hair as well. As a small boy, Nicholas had once tried to give himself a haircut with a pair of nail scissors and it looked as if Fiona had recently made a similar experiment.

'Fiona, this is Nicholas,' said Mr Fender. 'He's going to be in your class and I want you to look after him, make sure he knows his way around, has the things he needs and gets to wherever he's supposed to be going. Can you do that for me?'

Fiona nodded.

'Good. OK. On your way, both of you.'

Mr Fender watched as the two children headed off down the corridor and hoped he had done the right thing. He would not normally have asked a girl to look after a boy – he knew it could make both of them uncomfortable – but he thought it might be good for Fiona. He had been worried about her recently. She spent too much time alone, and she needed a friend.

He sighed as he went back into his office. He hoped Nicholas wouldn't be unkind or hurt her in any way. Fiona's life was quite difficult enough already.

Her appearance may have been a little strange, but Fiona looked after Nicholas very efficiently.

She took him to the English lesson with their form tutor, Miss Greco, made sure he got a copy of the textbook they were using, showed him what page they were on and lent him some file paper to take notes. At the end of the lesson, she took him along to French with Miss Barrie, and at break, she showed him where the toilets were before taking him to the library so that he could register, and take out the books he would need for Miss Greco's project. She was the sort of girl that teachers call *solid* and *sensible*, and there was something about the quiet, careful way she did all this that Nicholas rather appreciated.

He also appreciated the fact that, so far at least, there had been no accidents. In the English lesson, Miss Greco had tripped over a carpet tile and twisted her knee, but if that was the worst that happened, Nicholas thought, he could probably cope. As the librarian took his details and tapped them into the computer, he found himself fervently praying that the quiet would continue and that he would have a chance to settle in at Dent Valley.

When he rejoined Fiona, he found she was reading a book on first aid.

'It's for a test on Saturday,' she explained, when he asked. 'I was going over the four things to do when you discover someone unconscious.'

'There are four?' said Nicholas.

Fiona ticked them off on her fingers. '*Assess casualty's response. Open airways. Examine casualty for injuries and bleeding. Place in recovery position.*'

'I wish I'd known,' said Nicholas. 'Last time it happened to me all I could think of to do was shout "Help!"'

'You found someone unconscious?' Fiona sounded a little envious.

'I didn't exactly *find* him unconscious.' Nicholas still had vivid memories of the time the man collecting for Oxfam had called at their house. 'He sort of collapsed while I was talking to him, clutching his chest.'

'Ah, that sounds more like a heart attack,' said Fiona. 'You have to deal with them a bit differently.' She was ticking off her fingers again. '*Make the casualty comfortable. Dial 999. Monitor breathing. Then give them an aspirin to chew.*'

'An aspirin . . .' Nicholas picked up the book on first aid. 'Really?'

'You're welcome to read up about it.' Fiona glanced at the clock on the wall. 'But we'd better get moving. It's science with Mr Daimon next, and he can get very upset if people are late.'

The first of the accidents happened in Mr Daimon's class. It wasn't one of the bad ones – at least, not as bad as some of the things that had happened around Nicholas in the last eighteen months – but it was bad enough. And it dashed any hopes he might have had that life at Dent Valley was going to be different.

Mr Daimon was an energetic, quick-tempered man. His lesson that morning was on chemical reactions and the children were supposed to be measuring the different rates of reaction using various promoters and catalysts. He expected his students to take the work seriously and became very irritated if his teaching was interrupted.

Ten minutes into the lesson, he was getting particularly cross with a girl called Amanda, who had dropped a contact lens into the tube of ammonium chloride she was heating, when a pigeon flew in through the open window.

It did a quick circle round the classroom, causing a certain amount of noise and excitement as it did, and tried to fly out again only to run smack into a pane of glass. A twitter of concern ran around the class.

'All right,' said Mr Daimon, 'it's only a bird, calm down!'

But, as the pigeon continued to fly round the room, the class was anything but calm. Children screamed whenever the bird flew near them, and the more noise they made, the more frightened the pigeon became. Being frightened, it made messes and, as it flew, it dropped them everywhere. They landed in people's hair, on their clothes and on their work, which of course led to more screaming.

'Stop this!' Mr Daimon bellowed. 'Stop this noise at once! If I do not have silence this instant, I will . . .'

But the class never heard what Mr Daimon planned to do if he did not have instant silence, because at that moment the pigeon swooped low over his head and one of its feet caught in his hair. Mr Daimon gave a cry of surprise. He shook his head and his whole body in all directions in his efforts to shake it off, scattering papers and knocking over bottles as he did so.

When the bird eventually broke free, he found that one of the bottles was sulphuric acid and that it had splashed over his hands and down the front of his trousers. He stopped calling for everyone to stop shouting, and rushed over to a basin to turn on a tap. His hands were already beginning to sting rather painfully.

By now, the class was a bedlam of noise. One boy was running along the top of the benches trying to catch the pigeon. Most of the children were trampling over each other's bags, feet and fingers in an effort to get away from it. Fiona had taken the first-aid box from the wall and was attending to a girl who had cut her hand on some broken glass (*clean wound in running water; apply sterilized dressing; elevate injured limb*), when suddenly there was silence.

The headmaster had appeared in the doorway and everyone stopped. Even the pigeon settled on a bookshelf by the door. Mr Fender stared at the chaos around him. He looked at the children, at the spatterings of bird mess, at the broken glass on the floor – and at Mr Daimon, moaning quietly at the sink, with little tendrils of smoke drifting up from spots on his trousers.

'I want everyone to sit down,' he said firmly, 'and keep very quiet.'

There was a shuffling as everyone went back to their seats. When they were all in place, Mr Fender reached gently for the pigeon on the shelf, carried it to the window and let it fly away.

'If that's acid on your trousers,' he said, turning to Mr Daimon, 'I think you'd better go down to the staffroom and get changed.' He looked at the rest of the class. 'Has anyone else been injured?'

Fiona brought out the girl with the cut hand, who was sent with three others to be treated in the school office, and after that the headmaster sent six children to the cloakroom to wash the pigeon mess from their clothes. He told the rest of the class to go the library until lunchtime, and read.

Although Nicholas had not been hurt in any way, he was probably more upset by these events than the people who had. It was, he now realized, going to be the same story all over again. The accidents would happen at this school, just as they had at his last. Someone would eventually realize that he was the cause of them, and then he would be asked to leave. He was more disappointed at the thought than he could say.

At lunchtime, when Fiona offered to give him a tour of the school buildings, he didn't wait while she went to the cloakroom, but crept quietly away. She was a nice girl and, for her own safety, it would be best if he kept as far away from her, and everyone else, as possible.

In a quiet corner at the back of the main building, he found a set of steps leading down to the boiler room. Ignoring the sign at the top that said 'No Entry', he climbed down to the concrete floor at the base and sat with his back against the wall. From above came the sounds of other children laughing and shouting and, much as he would have liked to join them, he knew it was better if he stayed down here. With a sigh, he reached into his bag and took out the plastic box containing his packed lunch.

'You didn't have to run away.' Fiona was standing at the top of the steps, looking distinctly hostile. 'If you didn't want to be with me, you could have said.'

Nicholas stared up at her.

'I'm supposed to be making sure you know where to go. Mr Fender said. And if you don't, I get into trouble.'

'I . . . I'm sorry . . .'

'What are you doing down there anyway?'

Nicholas opened his mouth to answer and then closed it again. What could he say? How could he explain that he was keeping away from Fiona and everyone else so that he didn't hurt them? And in trying not to hurt Fiona, he had hurt her anyway. It seemed that whatever he did, he couldn't win.

'It wasn't that I didn't want to be with you,' he said. 'I was trying to protect you.'

'Protect me?' Fiona stared at him. 'From what?'

'From . . .' Nicholas struggled to find the right words. 'From getting hurt.'

'Why would I get hurt?' Fiona had begun walking down the stairs.

'Because that's what happens to people when I'm around.'

'They get hurt?'

Nicholas nodded.

'But why?' Fiona came and sat down on the concrete beside him. 'I mean . . . why?'

And perhaps because he was tired, or perhaps because he no longer cared whether it was a secret or not, or perhaps simply because Fiona's was the first friendly face he had seen in some while, Nicholas found himself telling her about the curse. He told her about going to Spain on holiday, about what he had done to the grave of Toribio de Cobrales and how, from that day on, he had attracted misfortune and calamity.

He told her how the only reason he was still alive was that Señor Herez's grandmother had woven a protective shield round him. He told her about flying home from Spain, and he had just started telling her about the accidents that meant he had to leave his first school, when a voice called from the top of the stairs.

'What are you two doing down there?'

It was Mr Daimon. He had bandages on both his hands, which had been burned by the acid, and was wearing tracksuit bottoms instead of his trousers.

'This area's out of bounds; you ought to know that.' He was clearly in a bad mood, and peered angrily into the gloom at the base of the stairs. 'Fiona? Fiona Gibbon? Is that you?'

He leant forward with his hand on the stair rail but, with the burns and the bandages, realized too late that he was unable to get a real grip. His hand slid forward, his body followed and a moment later he was rolling in an ungainly series of somersaults to the bottom of the steps, where his head landed with a smart crack on an old brick lying among a pile of dead leaves.

He lay there, quite still.

Fiona moved quickly to the fallen body and lifted the head a fraction. She ran her fingers over the back of Mr Daimon's scalp and they came away smeared with blood.

'*First priorities,*' she muttered quietly to herself. '*Control blood loss and arrange transport to hospital.*' With one hand cradling the science teacher's head, she reached into her bag for a games shirt. 'You'd better go and tell someone to call an ambulance, Nicholas.'

Nicholas did not move. He had seen a lot of accidents in the last year and a half, but something about the speed and suddenness of this one left him paralysed.

'Nicholas!' Fiona repeated. 'You have to go and get help!' She had clamped the games shirt over the wound with one hand and was pointing up the stairs with the other. 'If you don't, he could . . .'

She stopped. Standing at the top of the steps was a policewoman.

WPC Hillshaw was visiting Dent Valley to give a lecture on road safety. She had recently transferred from an area of London where violence by pupils towards staff was not uncommon. When she saw Mr Daimon lying on the ground and two children beside him, one of them with blood on her hands, she jumped to what seemed the obvious conclusion.

'Don't move!' She was already reaching for her truncheon and a can of mace. 'Don't either of you move a muscle!'

'WPC Hillshaw,' said the headmaster, 'would like to apologize.'

Mr Fender was sitting in his office, with the children opposite him, and WPC Hillshaw standing beside him, looking slightly embarrassed.

'Yes,' she said stiffly. 'I would indeed. I was far too hasty at lunchtime today. Only when I saw you, and the blood and everything, I assumed that . . .'

'It's all right,' said Fiona. 'We quite understand.'

'And if I was a bit heavy-handed with the wrist restraints,' WPC Hillshaw continued, clenching her fists nervously, 'I apologize again. If you want to make a formal complaint, I shall quite understand and –'

'No, no,' Nicholas interrupted her. 'That won't be necessary.'

Fiona nodded her agreement. 'We know you were only doing your job.'

'That's very understanding of you.' WPC Hillshaw relaxed a little. 'Thank you.'

It was nearly three hours since Mr Daimon had fallen down the steps and a good deal had happened in that time. An ambulance had arrived and taken him to hospital, and Nicholas and Fiona had both been arrested for attempted murder.

Nicholas's mother had been called to the school where she found her son sitting in handcuffs in the back of a police car, while other officers tried to contact Fiona's father who, perhaps fortunately, had gone out for a walk.

Mr Daimon recovered consciousness on the way to the hospital and was able to explain that his fall had been an accident but, by the time the news got back to the school, there were eleven policemen scattered over the school grounds doing everything from forensic analysis to photographing the scene of the crime. It was gone four o'clock before everything was sorted out and back to normal.

'I gather Mr Daimon will want to thank you as well,' said the headmaster. 'The doctor at the hospital said the way you stopped the bleeding from the wound in his head quite possibly saved his life.'

Fiona blushed modestly. She had, Nicholas noticed, taken this whole affair much more calmly than he'd expected.

'I've got a police car outside ready to take you home,' said WPC Hillshaw. 'In the circumstances, it's the least I can do.'

At the headmaster's suggestion, the children went to have a wash and clean-up first. Walking along the corridor to the cloakrooms was the first time they had been alone together since the accident, but for several minutes neither of them spoke.

It was Fiona, with her hand on the door to the girls' cloakroom, who finally broke the silence.

'Things like that happen to you all the time?' she said.

'Like I told you,' Nicholas answered, 'I am the unluckiest boy in the world.'

CHAPTER FOUR

After all that had happened, Nicholas half expected that Fiona would never want to speak to him again, but he was wrong. She gave him a little wave as he came into the classroom the next morning and indicated that he come and sit beside her.

'How's it going?' she asked as he sat down. 'Anything happened today yet?'

'There was a traffic accident while I was walking in,' said Nicholas, 'but only a small one. Nobody hurt.'

The accident had happened when a squirrel leapt out of a tree as Nicholas walked past, landing on the head of a cyclist who swerved off the road into a hole where they were repairing the drains. He could not be entirely sure that he had been the cause, but he thought it likely. Animals tended to behave strangely when he came near them.

'Do you think anything will happen at school today?' asked Fiona.

Nicholas admitted that it was probable.

'Though I doubt if it'll be anything as bad as yesterday,' he added. 'When there's been a major disaster like that, things usually calm down a bit for a few days. All the same, I think it might be best if I keep away from you. I'll go and sit the other side of the room . . .'

Fiona, however, would not hear of him moving anywhere. The fact that being close to Nicholas might involve her in further accidents did not seem to worry her at all.

'If anything does happen,' she said, 'I've brought this.'

She produced a large box marked with a green cross from her bag.

'It's got most of the things we might need.' She opened the lid to show him. 'Sterile dressings, bandages, disposable gloves, face shield, cleansing wipes . . . Dad gave it me for Christmas two years ago, but I've never had a chance to use it yet.'

Nicholas could not help but admire the very positive attitude she seemed to be taking. He hoped it was not something she would come to regret.

In fact, there were only two accidents that morning. One was in maths, when a fly flew up the nose of Mr Pierce just as he was opening a packet of drawing pins, resulting in a punctured knee when he knelt down to pick them up off the floor. And the other was in RE, when Miss Rawlins was knocked unconscious by thirty-six copies of the *Good News Bible* that slid off the shelf above her desk and fell on her head. At least Nicholas knew what to do about it this time. If someone was unconscious, he remembered, you stood back and let Fiona deal with it – which she did with great efficiency.

At lunchtime, the two children strolled across the playing field to find somewhere quiet to eat their sandwiches, and Nicholas showed Fiona how any plant or flower that he touched would wither and die. Her eyes widened at the sight of the grass blackening beneath his hand when he ran his fingers over the ground, and the daisy that closed and shrivelled up when she held its petals against his arm.

'Isn't there anything you can do about it?' she asked. 'I mean, can't you find someone to help?'

'We've tried.' Nicholas gave a sigh. 'But the only time we found anyone who said they knew what to do, they were hit by the curse before they could do anything.'

He told Fiona about the woman from the north, who had been knocked down by a lump of ice on her way to the front door.

'Ice fell out of the sky?' said Fiona. 'Where from?'

Nicholas shrugged. 'I've no idea.'

'Do things fall out of the sky very often?'

Nicholas thought about it. 'It's happened a few times. At my last school, on sports day, some fish fell out of the air into the swimming pool.'

'Fish?'

Nicholas nodded. 'They think it was caused by freak atmospheric conditions in France. Most of them were lampreys, but one was a baby crocodile and it gave the relay team some nasty nips.'

He rather enjoyed being able to talk to someone about all the strange things that had happened to him, and the wonderful thing about talking to Fiona was that none of the stories seemed to worry or frighten her. She was interested, particularly if they involved some sort of medical crisis, but never upset, and the fact that she could listen so calmly to descriptions of the most extraordinary events made her a very relaxing person to be with.

The one thing that did worry Nicholas was that spending time with Fiona made it more likely, if not inevitable, that she would one day be hurt by the curse herself. He liked her. She was the first real friend he had had in over a year, and the last thing he wanted was to see her get hurt. It was bad enough when things happened to people you didn't know. When they happened to people you liked and cared about, it was ten times worse.

Fortunately, for the next two days at least, nothing did happen to Fiona. Some things happened to other people in their class – Amanda Dowling set fire to her hair with a bunsen burner, and Tom Rattan stapled his ear to a bit of cardboard – but neither of the injuries were serious. Fiona provided first aid for both of them, and the calm, methodical way in which his friend did what was necessary made Nicholas admire her even more.

The two children came to spend almost all their time together. They sat together in class, spent break times talking or walking together through the grounds and, at the end of the week, Fiona asked Nicholas if he would like to come home with her for tea.

'Well, I'd like to,' said Nicholas, 'you know I would, but I'm not sure it'd be wise. Suppose the accidents start happening there?'

'If they do,' said Fiona, 'we'll just have to manage. Like your mum does in your house.'

She had recently, Nicholas noticed, had her hair cut – possibly by someone with a pair of garden shears – in a way that made it look even worse than before.

'And I want you to meet my dad,' Fiona went on. 'I think you'd like him.'

She was very insistent and, in the end, Nicholas gave way. In truth, he did not need a great deal of persuasion. He had been without friends for so long that the thought of spending time after school with someone that he liked was almost irresistible.

Fiona lived on the ground floor of a small block of flats in Carlton Place, near the railway station. She had her own key and, as she opened the front door, called out, 'It's me, Dad. I'm home!'

Mr Gibbon had been confined to a wheelchair ever since a motorcycle accident that happened when Fiona was only two years old – the same accident in which her mother had unfortunately been killed. He had, nevertheless, brought up his daughter entirely on his own for the next ten years, though recently the roles had been slightly reversed when he started losing his sight.

Mr Gibbon had an eye disease called *retinitis pigmentosa*, which is caused by a defective gene. His eyesight had been adequate for most of his life, but about a year ago had suddenly deteriorated, leaving him first with tunnel vision and then almost totally blind. It meant that, these days,

Fiona looked after him at least as much as the other way round.

Despite all this, he was a remarkably jolly-looking man. He was short and round, with a cheery smile on his face and long dark hair pulled back in a ponytail, was dressed in a faded pair of jeans with a T-shirt that had 'I love my Harley' written on the front. He gave Fiona a hug as she bent down to kiss him.

'This is Nicholas, Dad,' she said as she stood up. 'The boy I was telling you about.'

'So you're the lad who's been looking after my daughter, eh?' Mr Gibbon held out his hand. 'Pleased to meet you.'

Nicholas wasn't sure why Mr Gibbon should think he had been looking after Fiona when it had so obviously been the other way round, but he shook hands and murmured something polite.

'How are you enjoying school?' asked Mr Gibbon.

'It's not too bad,' said Nicholas.

'Never liked it much myself,' said Mr Gibbon. 'Mind you, schools were very rough places in my time. I remember our headmaster used to beat everyone at least once a day, including the staff, and if you did anything serious, like talking out of turn, they'd hang you up by the ankles with barbed wire and cut bits of your ears off.'

'Dad!' said Fiona.

'Quite right. Mustn't exaggerate.' Mr Gibbon smiled at Nicholas. 'Forget the barbed wire. They used ordinary rope most of the time.' He swung his chair round and headed out for the kitchen. 'I'm doing a spaghetti Bolognese for supper. I hope you're not a vegetarian!'

Nicholas followed Fiona and her father out to the kitchen where a saucepan was bubbling on the stove.

He stared around in some curiosity. 'How do you cook when you can't see?' he asked.

'Very carefully,' said Mr Gibbon, with a chuckle. 'And I make quite a lot of mess even then. Here, I'll show you round.'

The kitchen had been set up very differently to the one Nicholas had at home. The sink and the work surfaces were set at a lower height, so Mr Gibbon could reach them from his chair, and there were all sorts of gadgets he used to make up for the fact that he couldn't see what he was doing. There were talking jugs and scales to measure ingredients. There was a device you put in saucepans to tell you when the contents were boiling, and something called a liquid-level indicator that made a beeping noise when you'd filled your cup or glass.

While Mr Gibbon was explaining the importance

of putting tins in the right place so you knew which ones to open, Fiona made a pot of tea and set out biscuits and cups on a tray. She carried it back to the sitting room, and she and Nicholas sat at the table and did their homework while Mr Gibbon played the piano.

He was a remarkable pianist. He played without music and his short pudgy fingers darted over the keys with astonishing speed, moving gently from one tune to another. He seemed to know hundreds of songs and to be able to play any tune you mentioned. Once homework was finished, Nicholas found himself sitting beside him at the piano singing along to some of them while Fiona laid the table for supper.

It was a very pleasant evening. At first, Nicholas found it difficult to enjoy it as freely as he would have liked. He was nervous, and a part of him was waiting anxiously for something bad to happen. But for some reason it never did, and as time went by he almost forgot about it. At six o'clock they had supper in the kitchen, washing down the spaghetti with bottles of Coke, then Mr Gibbon produced a fruit pudding he had prepared earlier, and after Fiona and Nicholas had done the washing-up, they all sat down to watch a television comedy about three nuns and a fitness instructor marooned on a desert island. Then they played poker using special cards with little bumps on the face, so that Mr Gibbon could read what they were, and matches as money to bet with. By the end of the game, Nicholas had won a hundred and forty-two matches and was feeling rather pleased with himself.

And still nothing had happened.

At eight o'clock, when his mother arrived, Mr Gibbon offered to drive them all home on his motorbike, which rather alarmed Mrs Frith until she realized it was a joke. She thought it was another joke when he said how nice it had been to have Nicholas to visit and was astonished to find that it wasn't. Mr Gibbon came to the door to wave them off, told Nicholas to be sure and call again soon, and he promised that he would.

Walking home, Mrs Frith asked how the evening had gone and Nicholas told her about the piano-playing and Mr Gibbon's kitchen and the poker.

'And there weren't too many . . . accidents?' she asked when he had finished.

'There weren't any,' said Nicholas.

'What? None at all?'

Mrs Frith was understandably surprised. A whole evening with other people without accidents was extremely rare. So rare she couldn't remember the last time it had happened.

They say a parent is only as happy as their saddest child, and life for Mrs Frith, since that day on the mountainside in Spain, had not been easy. She had lost her job, she had lost her friends, she had had to cope with innumerable accidents in her home and to the people around her – but the hardest thing had always been to watch what the curse had done to Nicholas. To see how difficult life was for him and how lonely it made him.

And now, here he was, smiling, humming a tune under his breath, and looking as if he hadn't a care in the world. He had been out with a friend, enjoyed himself, and come home again. It was what a lot of children did every day of their lives but she had not seen Nicholas do it in a long time.

'No accidents at all, eh?' she said. 'Well, that *is* good!'

And Nicholas agreed that it was very good indeed.

CHAPTER FIVE

Mr Fender was in his office, filling in an insurance claim, when the phone rang. 'Tom?' said the voice. 'It's Alan Bartlett. From King Edward's.'

Mr Fender recognized the speaker immediately. Alan Bartlett was the head of a secondary school on the other side of town. They had met on various occasions, though not recently. In the last year, Mr Bartlett's school had been facing a series of problems that had kept its head extremely busy.

'How are you?' asked Mr Fender. 'And how's the rebuilding going?'

One of the difficulties Mr Bartlett had been dealing with was the loss of one of his classroom blocks in a freak tornado.

'Slowly,' said Mr Bartlett. 'Look, I'm ringing

because I heard you've taken on a new student. Nicholas Frith. Is that right?'

'Yes, we have. Joined us a week ago. He seems a nice enough lad.' Mr Fender suddenly remembered something he had read in Nicholas's file. 'Of course! He was with you for a term, wasn't he?'

'Six weeks. That was all I could take.'

'Really?' Mr Fender leant forward at his desk. 'You're telling me he's some sort of trouble-maker?'

Headmasters often tell each other, unofficially, if a student living locally is likely to cause difficulties.

'Have you had any accidents recently?' asked Mr Bartlett.

'Well, nothing as bad as your tornado, or the food poisoning,' said Mr Fender, 'but yes, we have had a few. Little things mostly. Like this morning our head of IT slipped on a packet of aniseed balls and cracked his head on an Apple Mac. I'm giving them a talk in assembly tomorrow on how we've got to be more safety conscious.'

'It won't do any good,' said Mr Bartlett.

'Why not?' Mr Fender frowned. 'What do you mean?'

There was a long pause before the headmaster of King Edward's answered.

'I know you won't believe this, but I'm going to tell you anyway. It's Nicholas. He's the one causing the accidents. They all happen because of him. I didn't believe it myself at first, but in the end I had no choice. I told him he had to leave and I suggest you do the same.'

'But Nicholas can't be causing the accidents here.' Mr Fender ran his mind over some of the things that had happened in the last week. 'He can't be. And why would he want to anyway?'

It sounded as if Alan was cracking up under the strain. He was a young and brilliant teacher, but the pressures of responsibility can get to the best of minds.

'He doesn't want to cause them, but he does,' said Mr Bartlett. 'And before you think I'm cracking up, talk to Marjorie. Marjorie Parkes. See what she says. She had him for a whole term.' There was another pause. 'Take my advice and get rid of him, Tom. Get rid of him before it's too late.'

There was a click, and the phone went dead as he hung up.

Fiona and Nicholas arrived for their science lesson after break to hear Mr Daimon announce that he was giving the class a revision test on the work they had done so far that term. When

Nicholas put up a hand to ask if he had to take the test as well, he got a very short reply.

'Of course you do,' Mr Daimon snapped. 'Now sit down and keep quiet.'

Fiona saw that Nicholas was looking worried and tried to reassure him. 'He knows you weren't here for the start of term,' she said. 'He won't expect you to do very well.'

Nicholas explained that doing well was not what he was worried about. 'I can't do tests,' he told her in a low voice. 'It's in the curse. *May he fail in any test or trial.* I can't do them!'

'Why?' Fiona looked concerned. 'What happens if you do?'

'If I don't have complete silence,' said Mr Daimon sharply, 'this entire class will find itself in detention.'

There was a slight delay when he discovered that the test papers he had prepared had somehow fallen into the sink where a leaking tap had made them all but illegible, but he was determined to carry on. He told the class he would write the questions on the board and they could do their answers on sheets of paper, and he had got as far as copying out the second question, when a wasp flew in the window.

The windows in Mr Daimon's classroom were only open a fraction – so that there could be no repeat of the pigeon incident – but the gap was easily big enough for the wasp to get in. It was a noisy insect and, after it had buzzed busily around the classroom for a minute, it was joined by another. And then a third, and then a fourth . . .

By the time Mr Daimon became aware that something was wrong, there were a dozen wasps buzzing around the classroom and more of them pouring in through the window every second. He opened a window to try and let them out, but all that happened was that more of them flew in. He shouted at the children to keep calm and not make a fuss, but most of them were too busy swatting at the wasps with exercise books and rolled-up pieces of paper to hear him.

A lot of the wasps seemed to be gathering round Mr Daimon's head as he stood at the window. Several landed on his face and one of them stung him on the forehead. He opened his mouth in a cry of pain and another one flew inside and stung him on the tongue. He had wasps climbing up his trouser legs, more crawling inside the buttons of his shirt and, in a sudden blind panic, he ran for the door, abandoning his classroom, and went racing off down the corridor with a stream of wasps in his wake.

Moments later, the insects disappeared as rapidly as they had arrived, but not before they had done a good deal of damage. Most of the children had received at least one sting – one boy had six just on his arm – and Fiona was extremely busy looking after them, removing the stings by scraping them off sideways with a fingernail and applying cold compresses.

She suggested that Nicholas go and make sure Mr Daimon was all right.

'I think I saw him stung in the mouth,' she said, 'which can be quite serious. The swelling might close up his windpipe, and there's the possibility of anaphylactic shock.'

Mr Fender sat in his office, staring thoughtfully at the phone on his desk. He had just had the most extraordinary conversation with the head teacher of St John's. Marjorie Parkes was a tough, no-nonsense teacher of the old school, now nearing retirement. Somehow, hearing a woman like Marjorie say what she had about Nicholas had made the whole thing seem even more bizarre.

'Alan's right,' she had barked. 'The boy's a Jonah. You have to get rid of him, and the sooner the better.'

'But I don't understand!' Mr Fender was still trying to come to terms with what he was being told. 'How *can* he be causing these accidents?'

'Does it matter?' Marjorie Parkes answered

briskly. 'There was a rumour, when he was here, that he was under some sort of curse, but I never cared if it were true or not. I just didn't want the ambulance turning up at the main gates twice a day. Has anyone tried to give him a test yet?'

'I . . . I don't know . . .'

'Well, don't let them. That's one way of guaranteeing that the dirt hits the fan. I'm telling you, Tom, you need to get him out of there. Bad things happen when that boy's around.'

'But I can't just throw him out,' Mr Fender protested. 'Not without a reason.'

'You don't need a reason. You call in his mother and tell her to take him away. I told her if she didn't, I'd plant the drugs in his pocket myself. One way or another, I said, he has to go.'

'You . . . you threatened to plant drugs on him?'

'I'd have done it too.' Miss Parkes's voice dropped to a quieter level for a moment. 'You can't have him in your school, Tom. Believe me, too many people get hurt.'

For some time after the call, Mr Fender sat in his chair, wondering what on earth he should do. He was still wondering, when Mrs Lear, the deputy head, brought him the news about Mr Daimon and the wasps.

'Wasps?' The headmaster could hardly believe his ears. 'In January?'

'Perhaps it was waking too early that made them so aggressive,' suggested Mrs Lear. 'Thankfully the children are OK, but we've had to send Michael to hospital again, I'm afraid. Forty-three separate stings, poor fellow. He's not having a lot of luck at the moment, is he?'

'No,' Mr Fender agreed, and then, as his deputy turned to leave, he asked, 'You don't happen to know what he was teaching them, do you?'

'In science?' Mrs Lear thought for a moment. 'I think one of the children said they were doing a test.'

'Were they,' murmured Mr Fender. 'Were they really . . .'

It was too cold to go outside and Fiona and Nicholas spent their lunch break in the library.

'So,' said Fiona, 'is that what happens every time you try and take a test?'

'More or less.' Nicholas was feeling rather gloomy. 'I've never had the wasps before, but there's always something that stops me.'

'Well, you shouldn't let it upset you.' Fiona had never done very well in school tests and the thought of not being able to take one seemed, if anything, rather attractive. 'I mean, who wants to do tests anyway?'

'It might sound OK,' said Nicholas, 'but

what's going to happen when I get older? What's going to happen if I can't pass any exams, or get any qualifications, or get a licence to drive a car?'

He had a point, Fiona realized. Not being able to pass any test or exam at all could have serious disadvantages as you grew up. She thought about it, on and off, for the rest of the day, and it was as they were walking home together after school that she wondered if there might not be a way out.

'Do you know how long it is,' she asked, 'before the curse takes effect? I mean, how long is there between sitting down to take a test and something bad happening?'

Nicholas said it varied but was usually very quick. In Mr Daimon's science lesson, he pointed out, the wasps had started coming in the window before he had written up even the first two questions.

'Yes, but they were quite long questions, weren't they?' said Fiona. 'And some people had written the answer to the first one by then.'

Nicholas said he thought it didn't make a great deal of difference if the disaster happened at once or five minutes later, it was still a disaster.

'But supposing it was a really short test,' Fiona suggested, 'and supposing you could answer all the questions really quickly and finished them before anything could happen? Wouldn't that mean you'd broken the curse? And if you'd broken it once, wouldn't that mean it was losing its power over you?'

Nicholas thought about it and found the idea very appealing. He did not know if finishing a test would weaken the curse but, whether it did or not, it would be very good to know that he had beaten it, even once.

'It would have to be a very short test,' he said.

Fiona had already thought of that. In the first lesson on a Thursday, Mr Galt gave the class a French vocab test. He showed them twenty words that he had already written on the whiteboard and gave everyone two minutes to write down what they meant in English.

'If you knew it really well,' said Fiona, 'you could probably do it in half the time.'

He probably could, Nicholas thought, and it was very tempting. The prospect of winning even a tiny victory against the curse that had blighted his life for more than a year and a half was hard to resist.

Nicholas knew that the faster he could write down the answers, the more chance there was of success, so he prepared for the test very carefully. That evening, he and Fiona went over all the words they were supposed to know several times. It took them over an hour, and they did the same thing the following evening and again the evening after that.

'You want to be careful,' Mr Gibbon warned them cheerfully. 'A boy at my school tried to work that hard and his brains overheated and came dribbling out of his nose.'

By the time Thursday arrived, Nicholas knew the vocab so completely that he could have passed the test in his sleep. At the start of the lesson, however, he ran into an immediate snag, when Mr Galt told him he was not allowed to take it.

'The headmaster,' he explained, 'has told the staff you're not to do any tests or exams. Why don't you read a book till we've finished?'

'I don't want to read a book!' protested Nicholas. 'I want to take the test!'

'Well, I'm sorry.' Mr Galt was already walking away. 'Mr Fender was very definite.'

'But that's not fair!' Fiona stepped in to give Nicholas support. 'He's been working for this test for days. Why can't he take it?'

Mr Galt hesitated. He was not entirely sure why the headmaster had said Nicholas should not take any exams or tests. Mr Fender had said something about the boy being sensitive, and reacting badly to pressure, but you only had to look at him to see how keen he was. Maybe, as it was only a little vocabulary test . . .

'All right,' he agreed, 'you can do it. But if you find it too difficult, or it upsets you for any reason, promise me you'll stop.'

Nicholas said that he would and triumphantly picked up his pen.

As Mr Galt revealed the words on the board and the test began, he scribbled down the answers as fast he could, keeping one eye open for anything strange that might be happening in the class around him.

There was a scratching sound from the book cupboard that made him a little uneasy. Then there was a thud as a large bird ran into the window (which he and Fiona had been careful to close before the lesson started) and a moment later there was a power cut, but Mr Galt ignored it, and the test was allowed to continue.

As Nicholas was writing the answer to question twenty, there was a loud bang, the cap flew off one of the radiators that ran along the wall under the window and a gush of scalding steam filled the room. The classroom had to be evacuated, of course, but he and Fiona managed to dash round first and collect up the answer papers, and it was with real pleasure that Nicholas watched Mr Galt carry them off to the staffroom to mark.

Mr Fender spent most of that morning talking to heating engineers and reorganizing the school timetable. The exploding radiator meant there was no heating in six classrooms and he had been told it would be several days before the fault could be repaired. In the meantime he had to find alternative places for Mr Galt and five other teachers to have their lessons.

It was not until lunchtime that he was able to talk to the French teacher and ask if it was true that, against his explicit instructions, he had allowed Nicholas Frith to take a test. Mr Galt explained that it had only been a little vocab test and Mr Fender told him firmly that, however small, he did not want Nicholas to take any tests in the future.

When Mr Galt asked why, Mr Fender pretended not to hear. He could not give the real reason; it sounded too absurd. But, absurd or not, he was determined not to risk another disaster.

'Out of interest,' he said as Mr Galt stood up to leave, 'how did Nicholas do in the test?'

'I'm afraid I don't know.' The French teacher blushed slightly. 'His paper was destroyed.'

'Destroyed?'

'In the staffroom. It caught fire.'

Mr Galt had carried the test papers to the staffroom and placed them on a window sill with his glasses on top. The sun had been shining and, as luck would have it, it had focused its beam through the lens, on to the paper beneath, and set fire to it. Only the top sheet had been destroyed before someone noticed, but that sheet had been Nicholas's.

'It's a shame,' Mr Galt said as he left, 'because he and Fiona had obviously worked very hard, and if her test is anything to go by, he'd have done very well.'

'Fiona?' Mr Fender looked up. 'Fiona did well?'

'Extremely well.' Mr Galt nodded. 'She got a hundred per cent.'

'A hundred per cent!' Mr Gibbon peered at the paper he was holding. He could not see the numbers, but he ran his fingers admiringly over the page. 'And top of the class, you say?'

'She was the only one with full marks,' said Nicholas. 'The boy who came second got ninety-five.'

'A hundred per cent . . .' Mr Gibbon was beaming from ear to ear. 'And what does it say at the bottom?'

'It says "Brilliant work! Well done!"' said Fiona, for the fourth time.

'Brilliant work . . .' murmured Mr Gibbon. 'I'll say it was. Well, I think this calls for a celebration.' He turned to his daughter. 'Why don't you ring up the Pizza Palace and get them to send round whatever you want!'

Fiona went out to the hall to make the call and Mr Gibbon sat in his chair, still chuckling to himself.

'A hundred per cent . . .' He leant forward and patted Nicholas on the knee. 'And all thanks to you, eh!'

'Me?' said Nicholas.

'Well, she wouldn't have done it without you, would she? All that revision you did together, that's why she did so well. I've been telling her for years she can do it if she puts her mind to it, but she wouldn't believe me.' Mr Gibbon leant back in his chair. 'We've got a lot to thank you for, Fiona and me. First you cheer her up by being her friend at school and now you're sorting out her work.' He touched the paper in his hand again. 'A hundred per cent! Who'd have thought it, eh?'

Nicholas was almost too astonished to speak. He had made things bad for the people around him for so long that it was almost impossible to believe he had done something this time that helped. He hoped with all his heart it might make up for anything bad that happened and the accidents he caused.

Not that anything bad had happened to either Fiona or her father yet, which, when he thought about it, was very odd. Nicholas had been going around with Fiona for nearly a fortnight now and, apart from being arrested for attempted murder that first day, she had not been involved in any accidents at all. Two weeks was a long time. Normally, the curse would have struck long before and a part of him wondered, nervously, how much longer the good times could last.

CHAPTER SIX

At registration the next morning, Miss Greco told Nicholas that the headmaster wanted to see him. He felt a slight tremor of foreboding, but Fiona assured him there was nothing to worry about. Mr Fender probably only wanted to ask how things were going, she said, and to check that he was settling in all right.

She was wrong.

'We need to talk,' said Mr Fender, pointing Nicholas to a chair. 'I was hoping to include your mother in this discussion, but when I tried to ring her this morning there was no reply.'

'No,' said Nicholas. 'The telephone line's down.'

The line was down because it had been hit by an Acme Thunderbolt firework, set off the night before by a man wanting to celebrate his divorce, but Nicholas thought it best simply to say that there had been an accident.

'An accident?' Mr Fender sniffed. 'Yes. We seem to be having a few of those recently, don't we?'

He reached into a drawer of his desk and took out a large exercise book.

'This is the record we keep of any injuries sustained on school premises,' he said, turning the pages, 'and you'll see that most weeks we have one or two, some weeks we don't have any . . . until a fortnight ago. Then we had twenty-nine accidents the first week, and this week we're already up to thirty-two.'

He pushed the book across the desk towards Nicholas.

'And you know the interesting thing? All the accidents happened to people who were some-how connected to you. We've got six teachers in there – all of whom teach you at one time or another – and almost all the other injuries are to children in your class. Do you have an explana-tion for that?'

Nicholas wondered how Mr Fender had worked it out so quickly. In both his last schools it had taken them much longer to make the connection.

'I was talking to Mr Bartlett yesterday, the head-master of your last school,' Mr Fender went on, 'and it seems there were a lot of accidents while you were there, as well. Then I rang Mrs Parkes at St John's, and it turns out she had the same trouble the term before.' Mr Fender leant back in his chair and looked carefully at Nicholas. 'So . . . what exactly is going on?'

Inwardly, Nicholas sighed. He should have known it was too good to be true. In the last two weeks, his life was actually starting to get better, he was almost beginning to enjoy himself and now . . . now it was all going to be taken away. The headmaster was going to ask him to leave, just as he had been asked to leave all his other schools. He should never have expected anything else.

'I asked you a question,' Mr Fender repeated. 'What is going on?'

'I . . . I can't explain,' said Nicholas.

'I think you can, and I think you'd better.' Mr Fender's voice was quiet but firm. 'It's my job to look after this school, and the people in it, and to do that I need to know about anything that might threaten them.'

He waited, but still Nicholas said nothing.

'Believe it or not, I'd like to help.' Mr Fender was speaking again. 'But I can't do that unless I know what the problem is, can I?'

'You couldn't help anyway,' said Nicholas in a low voice. 'Nobody can.'

'How about letting me decide that?' The headmaster's voice was stern, but his look was not unkind as he sat the other side of the desk, peering over the top of his glasses, waiting for an answer.

Nicholas made a sudden decision. It seemed to be one of those times when telling the truth could hardly make the situation worse. He was probably going to get thrown out anyway.

'All right.' He took a deep breath. 'If you really want to know, it began when I was on this holiday in Spain . . .'

At the same time as Nicholas was having his conversation with the headmaster, Mrs Frith was calling on Mr Gibbon.

She had been worried about him ever since the first day that she had picked up her son from the flat in Carlton Place and discovered that Mr Gibbon was disabled. It was wonderful that her son had found a friend who was prepared to take the risk of being with him, but it wasn't fair to include her father. Accidents were bad enough when they happened to ordinary, able-bodied people, but Fiona's father was in a wheelchair and almost completely blind. The sort of accidents he could have were too awful to think about.

In fact, she found it hard to believe that the

accidents weren't happening already. Her son had been round to the flat almost every evening that week and things *always* happened around Nicholas. They happened to anyone who was close to him and the more regularly he saw someone the more likely it was that the accidents would be bad ones. Nicholas insisted that nothing had happened yet and that Mr Gibbon was fine, but she needed to check for herself that it was true.

She knocked at the door of the flat in Carlton Place and, after a few minutes, it was opened by Mr Gibbon.

'It's me,' she said, 'Nicholas's mother. I was wondering if you had time to talk?'

'Well, I was about to practise my fire-juggling but, hey, I can do that any time.' Mr Gibbon spun his chair round and led the way through to the living room. 'Anything in particular you wanted to talk about? Dwindling earth resources, the decline of morals in young people . . .'

'It's Nicholas,' said Mrs Frith. 'I'm worried that his coming round here every evening might be making things difficult for you.'

'Difficult?' Mr Gibbon frowned. 'How do you mean?'

'Well . . .' Mrs Frith phrased her answer carefully. 'Sometimes things happen when a young boy comes into a house . . . you know . . . accidents.'

'You mean like all the accidents they've been having at school?'

'Yes,' said Mrs Frith. 'I wondered if anything like that was happening here as well.'

'Ah.' Mr Gibbon stroked thoughtfully at his chin. 'Well, we are a bit worried whether the baby wolf that bit Fiona yesterday had rabies . . .'

'Oh, goodness.' Mrs Frith paled. 'Nicholas never said anything about a wolf . . .'

'Of course he didn't!' Mr Gibbon chuckled. 'I was joking. No, we haven't had any accidents here. None at all.'

'You're sure?'

'Positive.'

Mrs Frith was finding it hard to believe. 'You mean that, when Nicholas comes round here, everything's normal?'

'Not normal, no.' Mr Gibbon smiled. 'Better than normal. He's been really good for Fiona.'

'He has?'

'He's been a good friend. Really perked things up for her. Even made her do some work.'

'So you . . . don't mind him coming round every day?'

'It's a pleasure to have him,' said Mr Gibbon happily.

'Well, I'm glad to hear it.' Mrs Frith was relieved, though still puzzled at the lack of accidents. 'I only wish there were something I could do in return.' She had a sudden thought. 'Perhaps there is. Perhaps I could offer to help with Fiona?'

'How d'you mean?'

'Well, I could take her to a hairdresser's for a start.' Mrs Frith smiled. 'I don't know who's cutting her hair at the moment but . . .'

'It's me,' said Mr Gibbon. 'I cut her hair. I've been doing it ever since she was little.'

'Oh,' said Mrs Frith. There was a slight pause before she asked, 'You don't buy her clothes as well, do you?'

'I certainly do. She tells me what she needs and I order it from the catalogue. I get Mrs Barnet from across the way to help fill out the form. You're not going to tell me there's something wrong with them as well, are you?'

Mrs Frith did not answer.

'Oh dear.' Mr Gibbon's normally cheery face had become a little downcast. 'That bad, is it?'

That evening, Mr Fender sat in his office staring out of the window until long after the children and staff had gone home. He was thinking, as he had been on and off all day, about the story Nicholas had told him. It wasn't easy to believe in a curse from a man who had been dead for three hundred years, not in this day and age, and yet . . .

And yet there had to be some explanation for the extraordinary things that had happened in his school during the last two weeks. Only that afternoon, Mrs Baker, Nicholas's history teacher, had had a seizure after inadvertently eating some laburnum seeds that had been blown by the wind into her yoghurt. And two girls in his class had superglued their shoulders together and been taken to casualty like a pair of Siamese twins. There was obviously something going on.

If a curse *was* causing the trouble, he wondered, what was he supposed to do about it? The simplest solution would be, as Alan Bartlett suggested, to ask Nicholas to leave, but something in Mr Fender rebelled against that idea. He was a head teacher, and a head teacher is responsible for *all* the children in his care. It was his job to look after the pupils at his school whatever their handicaps or disabilities. It might be a lot easier if he only had to deal with the children who didn't have problems, but he hadn't taken the job because it was easy.

But how *did* you help someone like Nicholas? If a child was dyslexic, or had rickets, or was deaf, there were experts he could call in to advise him. He had great lists of them in the filing cabinets round his office. But where did you go to find an expert on being cursed? Who could he possibly talk to?

Head teachers know a wide range of people. They teach the sons of dukes and the daughters of dustmen and, as part of their job, they meet people from almost every walk of life. Offhand, Mr Fender couldn't actually remember anyone who was an expert in curses, but there were one or two parents of past pupils who might be able to point him in the right direction. He remembered one mother who charmed warts and had offered to feng shui the classrooms. She might be a good place to start.

He reached for the phone.

That weekend, Mrs Frith took Fiona into town on something of a shopping spree. Mr Gibbon had drawn two hundred pounds from his bank account and told her to buy a complete new set of school clothes and anything else that might catch Fiona's eye.

It was something they very much enjoyed, at least they did once Mrs Frith had persuaded Nicholas to go for a walk and meet up with them later. Shopping with Nicholas was always difficult. Either the till wouldn't work, or the fire sprinkler system suddenly malfunctioned, or the assistant who was serving you ran off to chase a shoplifter. So they agreed to meet at McDonald's in two hours' time and, until then, Mrs Frith and Fiona were left to do their shopping in peace.

The trip was a new and exciting experience for Fiona. They bought two school skirts and blouses, some socks, a pair of shoes with the chunky square toes and big heels that everyone else was wearing and then, because there was still some money left, they went on to buy some jeans and a couple of vests from Topshop.

Finally, they went to the hairdresser's, where Fiona was given a haircut by a young man called Marco, who was dressed in a sort of romper suit covered in sequins but was very good at his job. When he had finished, Fiona was left staring into the mirror, not quite sure if the pretty girl staring back was really her. She wondered what Nicholas would say when he saw it but unfortunately, when they got to McDonald's, Nicholas had other things on his mind.

He had only been waiting by the door for a couple of minutes, but in that time two accidents had happened. First, a small fire had broken out in one of the waste bins, and then the manager, running out of his office to see why the smoke alarms had gone off, slipped on a patch of wet floor and somehow swallowed the button battery he had been trying to fit into his hearing aid.

Fiona instantly swung into action. She got Mrs Frith to use her mobile to phone the emergency services, told Nicholas to use the extinguisher on the wall to put out the fire in the bin, while she herself gave abdominal thrusts to the man who had swallowed the battery, making him cough it back out on to the floor. At the same time, she was giving instructions on looking after an old lady who had fainted at the sight of the fire, by telling her husband to lay her on the ground with her legs raised to improve the blood flow to her brain.

Mrs Frith watched it all with a deepening admiration. Nicholas had told her how calm Fiona was, even when the most extraordinary things were happening, but until now she had never quite believed it.

'She's done all these first-aid courses with the St John Ambulance.' The fire was out and Nicholas had come to stand beside his mother. 'She started doing them when her dad was going blind, so she'd know how to look after him if anything happened. Then she got sort of interested.' He looked down at his friend with a quiet pride. 'It's been really useful at school. Whatever happens, she always seems to know what to do. She's amazing.'

Mrs Frith was inclined to agree, and she was

beginning to think she might have been wrong to presume that Nicholas's friendship with Fiona could not last. The more she saw of her, the more it seemed that Fiona was exactly what he needed.

Mr Fender also had an errand in town that Saturday, though it was one he was hoping to keep secret if possible. He parked his car in the road outside a row of terraced houses and checked carefully that no one was watching before getting out and walking up to the door of number 47.

A part of him wondered what the local newspaper might make of a headmaster getting advice from a 'psychic consultant' on how best to treat one of the pupils at his school. They would probably demand that he lost his job, and who could blame them?

Even now, he wasn't at all sure he was doing the right thing. But he knew he had to do something. If things went on the way they were he might not have a school left by the end of term. He had spent most of the previous evening on the phone, following up leads and suggestions from a number of people, and several fingers had pointed him in the direction of the front step on which he was now standing.

If this was the only way to solve the problem, then this was what he would have to do. He rang the bell and, a moment later, found himself facing a tall woman, dressed in a sari, with astonishingly bright green eyes.

'Mr Fender?'

The headmaster nodded and smiled a little nervously. He had been told that Miss Murajee possessed some extraordinary powers and wondered if these included being able to read his mind.

'Only occasionally,' said Miss Murajee. 'Would you like to come in?'

CHAPTER SEVEN

'Miss Murajee has kindly agreed to look at your . . . um . . . your problem,' the headmaster said, drumming his fingers on the desk as he glanced across at Nicholas, 'and to give us the benefit of her advice. She's a psychic expert and might be able to help – if that's all right with you?'

Nicholas assured him that it was. He had no idea what a psychic expert was but, after eighteen months under the curse of Toribio, he was prepared to take help from anyone.

'The suggestion is,' Mr Fender continued, 'that Miss Murajee follows you round the school today and observes what happens. That way she'll get an idea of the sort of . . . accidents that occur.'

'I don't know if I'll be able to do anything.' Miss Murajee spoke in a strong, deep voice. 'But I'll be happy to try.'

'I've told the staff that she's doing a background assessment of your social skills. I think it would be wiser not to mention her real purpose. So she'll sit at the back of the class during your lessons and, at the end of the day, we'll meet back here and . . .'

The headmaster was interrupted by the phone ringing. He answered it, listened for a moment and then stood up.

'If you'll excuse me,' he said, 'that was the caretaker. It seems the toilets in the science block are backing up. I'll be as quick as I can.'

Nicholas wondered, as the headmaster left, if the toilets backing up were caused by the curse.

'It might just be coincidence,' said Miss Murajee. 'It's hard to tell. I've studied magic most of my life, but the connections aren't always easy to follow.' She took out a notebook. 'Can you tell me exactly what this curse said?'

Nicholas told her and, when he'd finished, Miss Murajee gave a low whistle.

'I'm surprised you're still alive after that lot.'

'I'm protected,' Nicholas explained. 'By a spell this old lady put on me.'

'Yes, I can see that.' Miss Murajee peered at

him briefly. 'So the people around you get it instead. That can't be easy for you.'

'No,' said Nicholas. 'It's not.'

'I know how you feel. I was under a curse myself once. It was meant to be a joke but I couldn't see or recognize the number nine for over a month and you wouldn't believe how inconvenient it was. Still . . .' Miss Murajee put away her notebook and stood up. 'Let's get started, shall we?'

'Started?'

'I presume you're supposed to be in a lesson of some sort. You just carry on as normal and I'll tag along behind. If I'm going to be any help, I need to see this curse in action.'

Nicholas led her out of the main building and along the path to the classroom where he was supposed to be having a French lesson. He wondered, as he went, if Miss Murajee knew what she was letting herself in for.

They were walking past the corner of the main building when some instinct made him stop and look up. He was in time to see a roof slate falling out of thin air, heading directly for Miss Murajee's head. He opened his mouth to shout a warning but . . . there was no need. Miss Murajee was already stepping to one side and the slate landed harmlessly on the tarmac beside her, where it shattered into a thousand splinters.

The head of an embarrassed builder peered over the edge of the roof two storeys above. 'Sorry,' he called. 'It slipped. You all right?'

Miss Murajee gave him a cheery wave and walked on without even breaking her stride.

'It's very kind of you to be concerned,' she said, 'but there's no need to worry. I can look after myself.'

It was just as well that Miss Murajee *could* look after herself, because that particular morning was not a good one. The first two lessons were peaceful enough, though one boy did manage to stab himself in the hand with a mathematical compass, but the double science after break was a lesson that Nicholas would never forget.

It was Mr Daimon's first day back since the incident with the wasps and he was not in a good mood. He had given out three red cards and a detention before the lesson even started, to children who thought it was funny to make buzzing noises as they came in. Then, as he stood behind his desk to announce the experiment they would be doing, one end of the fluorescent light above him came loose from the ceiling, swung down and smacked him smartly on the side of the head.

It looked for a minute as if he was going to be all right. He was dazed, but seemed to recover and told everyone to settle down and open their books. But then he told the class to get into their pyjamas as it was bedtime, and began taking off his jacket and shirt. When Fiona went over to stop him, Mr Daimon told her in confidence that he was Father Christmas.

Nicholas looked across at Miss Murajee, the only other adult in the room, to see if she was going to do something, but she sat there, making no move. He was debating whether he should go and get the headmaster when the door swung open and a mountain lion padded softly into the classroom.

For a moment, there was total silence, broken only by Mr Daimon asking if it was time for breakfast yet, but then he saw the lion and went very quiet as well.

Mountain lions are not normally seen strolling through classrooms in English schools. This one had escaped from a lorry that had overturned on the dual carriageway. It had been on its way to the zoo at Longleat, when the lorry crashed into the central reservation, and the lion, along with two zebras and a gnu, had got free.

It was not a particularly large animal, but it was powerfully muscled and with claws that tapped on the tiled floor as it walked. Like most wild creatures, it would probably not have attacked a human unless it felt threatened in some way and would most likely have gone back out the way it came in, if the wind hadn't banged the door shut so that it found itself trapped in the classroom. Its lip pulled back in a snarl and it started moving towards Mr Daimon.

As it did so, a voice rang out with a quiet but commanding authority.

'Nobody move!' It was Miss Murajee. 'Everyone stays exactly where they are and nobody moves a muscle.'

The classroom was frozen and the mountain lion took another couple of steps forward. It sniffed briefly at Mr Daimon's knees then lifted its head to look at Fiona with a slightly puzzled expression, as if it wasn't sure what it was supposed to do next.

At the back of the classroom, Nicholas became aware of a deep humming noise. It was a low continuous sound and, if Mrs Frith had been there, she would have recognized it as the same sound Señor Herez made in the back of the taxi on the journey down from the mountain. The humming came from Miss Murajee, who had come to stand beside Nicholas. The lion seemed to hear it too. It turned away from Fiona and Mr Daimon, and began walking down the aisle between the benches to the back of the class.

Behind it, Mr Daimon slid to the floor in a dead faint.

The humming noise continued without any interruption. Miss Murajee never stopped to take a breath and never took her eyes from the lion as it paced across the floor towards her. It stopped, directly in front of her, and so close that she could have reached out a hand to touch its head. Again, it had that puzzled, uncertain look. It blinked a few times, yawned and very slowly lay down on the floor and closed its eyes.

In the classroom, nobody dared even to breathe. The humming sound went on . . . and on . . . and then stopped.

'All right, everyone.' Miss Murajee was speaking very quietly. 'You can leave, but please make as little noise as possible. When you get out, find another classroom, close the door and stay there until someone tells you it is safe.'

As the children filed quietly of the room, Miss Murajee tapped Nicholas on the shoulder without taking her eyes off the lion. 'I want you to help Fiona with Mr Daimon, and wait for me outside.'

Nicholas tiptoed quietly past the lion, which raised its head for a moment to watch him through sleepy eyes, and walked over to Fiona, who was still kneeling by the unconscious Mr Daimon.

They each took one foot and dragged him into the corridor outside. It was completely empty, there was no one in sight, and they were wondering what to do next when Miss Murajee appeared, quietly closing the classroom door behind her.

'Well!' She dabbed at her forehead with a handkerchief. 'That was interesting!'

'What do we do now?' asked Nicholas.

'We wait.' Miss Murajee cocked her head to one side. 'It won't be long. They're on their way.'

A few minutes later, men came running down the corridor. They wore crash helmets with large visors, heavily padded clothing that covered every inch of their bodies, and carried an assortment of nets, poles with wire loops on the end, and rifles.

'Where is it?' asked one of the men.

'He's in there.' Miss Murajee pointed to the classroom. 'Asleep. If you go in quietly, I don't think he'll give you any trouble.'

Mr Fender had not known a day like it in nearly thirty years of teaching. His phone had been ringing non-stop for two hours, with parents wanting to know if their sons or daughters were still alive, or whether they had been savaged by an escaped lion. It couldn't go on, he thought. He simply couldn't let it go on.

'It's not as bad as you think,' said Miss Murajee. 'I'm afraid this morning was partly my fault.'

'Your fault?' Mr Fender blinked.

'I added my own powers to the curse for a while. So that I could see what was happening more clearly.'

'And . . . ?'

'As I said, it's not as bad as you think.' Miss Murajee sipped at a cup of tea. 'I would say that, with a few precautions, the problem could be contained and you could run this school in perfect safety.'

'Really?' Mr Fender looked at her doubtfully.

'The first thing to understand,' said Miss Murajee, helping herself to a biscuit from the plate on the desk, 'is how the curse works. It uses emotional energy, you see. It gathers its power from the anger and fear of the people around it. As I've explained to Nicholas, he's a sort of lightning conductor. He attracts the negative energy in the people around him and the curse uses that energy to create misfortune. I don't know if you've noticed, but the people who are harmed by Nicholas's presence are usually the highly strung, angry, emotional type.'

The headmaster thought that angry and emotional was a good description of Mr Daimon.

He was an excellent teacher but very easily upset by children not doing exactly what he wanted.

'And the people who *don't* get hurt are those who are, by and large, calm and accepting of the things that happen around them,' Miss Murajee went on. 'Nicholas's friend Fiona is a good example. She has almost no negative energy at all, and I suspect her father's the same. It's not a total protection by any means, but it's why fewer things happen to them than to others.'

Mr Fender nodded. It made a sort of sense.

'But what can I do? I can't make a rule that nobody's allowed to get angry whenever they're near Nicholas. It wouldn't happen . . .'

'But you could ensure that he was only taught by those teachers who were calmer and less emotional, couldn't you? And perhaps you could put him in a class with children who were more like Fiona and less . . . exuberant?'

'I suppose I could.' Mr Fender still sounded rather doubtful.

'The second thing I can suggest is that we make a Safe Room,' said Miss Murajee. 'My powers aren't strong enough to lift the curse itself, but I can create a small area where Nicholas would be immune to its effects. If you provided a small office or an old store cupboard, he would be able to go there on the bad days, when he sensed things were going wrong – and then everyone would be protected from him.'

'OK.' Mr Fender was making notes on a pad. 'I can manage that . . . Anything else?'

'The animals are the biggest risk,' said Miss Murajee. 'They're drawn to him, you see. They don't necessarily mean any harm but the reactions of the other children make them dangerous. I'd strongly suggest you set up some sort of alarm system, so the staff can call for help – and you really ought to have someone besides Fiona trained in first aid. Preferably two or three – and they need to have done courses in poisonous insects and venomous snakes.'

'Right . . .' Mr Fender had no idea how he was going to achieve this, but he wrote it down. 'And if I do all this, I won't have to keep sending my staff and pupils to hospital?'

'You'll be all right.' Miss Murajee leant across and patted his hand consolingly. 'Honestly. You'll be all right.'

Nicholas was relieved to hear that Mr Fender had decided to let him remain at the school for a further trial period, provided he followed Miss Murajee's advice, but the events of the morning had disturbed him more than he cared to admit.

In his mind's eye he could still see the mountain lion walking towards Fiona and Mr Daimon. Suppose that had happened while Miss Murajee was not there? What would he have done? The idea that his friend could have been badly hurt, and that it would have been his fault if she were, was not a pleasant one.

When Miss Murajee had finished giving him her instructions on how he was to behave in school in future, he asked if there wasn't anything else she could do.

'Like what?' asked Miss Murajee.

'You said you were under a curse once, and you got rid of it. Isn't there some way you can get rid of mine?'

'No,' she said firmly. 'I'm sorry. I can't do that.' Then she smiled. 'But cheer up. It could be worse!'

'Could it?' muttered Nicholas. 'I don't see how.'

'Of course it could,' said Miss Murajee briskly. 'I know life's not easy for you at the moment but that doesn't mean you have to go around looking so miserable.'

'I'm the unluckiest boy in the world,' said Nicholas. 'I don't have a lot to be happy about.'

'We don't need *reasons* to be happy,' said Miss Murajee firmly. 'Happiness isn't something that happens to you, it's a decision. So stop feeling sorry for yourself and start smiling.' She took out a card and gave it to him. 'That's my number. Any time you need me, give me a call.'

CHAPTER EIGHT

After that day with Miss Murajee, things did seem to get better, and the number of accidents happening around Nicholas was reduced dramatically.

Mr Fender had panic buttons installed in all the classrooms, connected to the school office. He sent four of his staff on training courses in first aid, and he altered the timetable, as Miss Murajee had suggested, so that Nicholas only had lessons with the more relaxed and easy-going members of staff. Mr Daimon was still away after the mountain-lion incident and Nicholas did science with Mrs Mackintyre, a large, middle-aged woman who never seemed to get upset about anything. His French teacher was replaced by the elderly Mr Dobson, and Mr Fender himself took over the lessons in RE.

Some children were moved out of his class. Two of the noisier and more excitable girls were replaced, for instance, by boys from another form whose hobby was collecting wild flowers, and the effect of these changes was soon apparent. Miss Murajee had said that the energy of the curse depended on the emotions of the people around Nicholas and, when the people around him were, by and large, calm and relaxed, the energy for real disaster was no longer there.

Some accidents still happened. There was an incident with a tarantula in a geography lesson that sparked a certain amount of hasty movement, and the number of light bulbs that failed or computers that crashed when Nicholas was around could still reach highly inconvenient levels but, when they did, he knew what to do. As soon as the accident rate threatened to get out of control or to produce an atmosphere of fear and distrust that the curse could feed on, Nicholas would quietly leave the class and head for the Safe Room.

The Safe Room was an old stationery cupboard a few doors down the corridor from Mr Fender's office. The boxes of paper and exercise books had been taken out and Miss Murajee had replaced them with a small armchair and a table. The day after her first visit, she returned to the school and spent several hours in the room making strange incantations while burning sweet-smelling herbs.

Nicholas noticed the difference as soon as he stepped through the door. That sense he had carried for the last eighteen months of malevolent forces swirling around him, waiting to pounce, disappeared in an instant. It was as if they could no longer see him. He was hidden from their view and, while he was hidden, both he and the people around him were safe.

It was a wonderful feeling. In fact it was so wonderful that a part of him wanted to stay in the room all the time, but Miss Murajee explained that would not be possible. Its power to shield him was limited, she said, and only to be used for an hour or so at a time on those occasions when he could feel the spiral of energy building up around him and needed some way to defuse it.

Even so, the effect on his life at school was dramatic. Within a matter of days, the number of accidents had dropped to something only slightly above what might be considered normal. When Miss Murajee called in, a week later, the headmaster was able to show her that, apart from Mr Daimon who was still in a convalescent home, he had a full complement of staff for the first time since Nicholas had joined the school. The only accidents in the last two days had been a couple of burst pipes and a girl in Nicholas's class who had swallowed a pencil sharpener.

He paid the bill for her services with the greatest pleasure. She was on the school books as a 'behavioural consultant' and to his mind she was worth every penny a thousand times over.

Perhaps the person who appreciated these changes more than anyone was Mrs Frith. For the last eighteen months, her life had been devoted to watching over Nicholas and dealing with the emergencies that arose so regularly in his life – and now all that had stopped, almost overnight. At first she could hardly believe it, but as the days went by she began to entertain the idea that the change might actually last.

She would see her son off to school in the morning, and not hear from him some days until six or seven in the evening, when he came back from the flat in Carlton Place. Maybe now was the time, she thought, for her own life to return to normal as well.

In the years before that fateful holiday in Spain, Mrs Frith had been the deputy manager of a Trust House Forte hotel a few miles outside town. It was a job she had enjoyed. She had loved the *busyness* of hotel life – the receptions, the conferences, the gala celebrations – as well as the people, the staff and the whole buzzing, humming energy of it all.

Having any sort of job, let alone working in a hotel, had been impossible while Nicholas was under the curse of Toribio, but now . . . now perhaps it was different. Within a week, Mrs Frith had applied for and been given the job of Reception Manager in the Royal Hotel in the centre of town, and she reported for her first day's work with unconcealed delight.

In view of how much she was looking forward to it, and how determined she was to do a good job, it was rather disappointing that she should have been fired on her second day.

'Fired?' Nicholas was almost as upset at the news as his mother. 'Why? What for?'

'I found one of the girls on the desk stealing money from the cash register,' Mrs Frith explained gloomily. 'I reported her to Mr Billings, the hotel manager, but he didn't do anything about it. When I told him I couldn't manage a reception where staff are allowed to steal from the till, he said in that case I'd better leave.'

So Mrs Frith had left, but she was very upset. Returning to work was something she had dreamed of for more than a year and, when it had finally happened, she had been dismissed after barely twenty-four hours.

Nicholas felt the injustice of it very keenly. He thought his mother should complain to someone, but she pointed out that Mr Billings was the manager, and there was no one else to complain *to*.

'She hadn't done *anything* wrong!' Nicholas protested to Fiona the next day. 'He actually fired her for doing the *right* thing. It's not fair!'

Fiona agreed and, at the end of the day, suggested that they call round at the hotel themselves before they went home. 'I think someone should complain,' she said. 'Even if your mother won't. Someone needs to tell Mr Billings that what he did was wrong.'

'It won't do any good, though, will it?' said Nicholas gloomily. 'I mean, it's not going to make him change his mind. He probably won't even listen.'

'Oh, I think he'll listen.' Fiona took her friend by the arm and led the way into town. 'You may not have noticed, but you have a way of getting people's attention.'

The Royal Hotel was a large, modern building, in a road just off the high street. Nicholas led the way through the main doors and across the hall to reception.

The girl at the desk had blonde hair, was painting her nails and did not look up as Nicholas explained that he had come to see Mr Billings.

'What for?' she asked, without lifting her eyes.

'I want to ask him why he made my mother lose her job,' said Nicholas, 'when all she did was report someone for stealing.'

The girl looked up and glared at him.

'The manager's not available,' she said. 'Sorry.'

'It's all right,' said Fiona. 'We'll wait until he is.' She took Nicholas over to a sofa on the other side of the hall where they sat down. The receptionist stared at them in hostile fury before returning to work on her nails.

'I'm not sure this is wise,' said Nicholas nervously. 'She looks really angry, and you know what happens when people get angry near me.'

'I think that's her problem, not yours,' said Fiona. 'All you're doing is waiting for a chance to see Mr Billings.'

They did not have to wait very long. A woman in a suit appeared from the lift, complaining that she couldn't get into her room because her key didn't work, and a moment later a man rang the desk to complain that he couldn't get *out* of his room because the door had locked itself.

The hotel used electronic locks, with keys looking rather like credit cards, and within minutes there were several other hotel guests in the lobby, all unable to get into their rooms, and all of them understandably annoyed. Not long after that, Mr Billings appeared to explain that there seemed to be a fault in the central computer that controlled the cards, but that he had called someone to come and fix it.

'That's him,' said Fiona. 'Go and have a talk to him now.'

A little nervously, Nicholas crossed the floor to Mr Billings.

'Could I ask you about my mother?' he asked.

'What?' Mr Billings spun irritably round to face him. 'Who are you?'

'I'm Nicholas,' said Nicholas, 'and my mother is Mrs Frith. You fired her yesterday, and I think it was very unfair. All she was doing –'

'I don't have time to talk to children!' Mr Billings interrupted angrily. 'I'm extremely busy. Please leave this hotel at once!'

'He's not leaving,' said Fiona, 'until you explain why his mother –'

'If you don't leave,' shouted Mr Billings, 'I shall throw you both out myself!' And he was actually reaching to grab Nicholas by the front of his shirt when there was a loud crash from outside. He ran to the doors in time to see a huge lorry slowly overturning in the driveway, depositing forty tons of gravel on the tarmac in front of the hotel, and completely blocking the entrance to the hotel car park.

While Mr Billings stared at the sight in horror, a waitress came in from the gardens to say that customers having tea on the terrace were complaining about the smell of dead fish coming from the ornamental pond, and what should she do?

Mr Billings did not answer. He was still staring, white-faced, out of the hotel at a man who was climbing over the mountain of gravel and making his way to the main doors.

'Mr Ryder . . .' The manager's mouth formed a sickly smile. 'This is an unexpected honour!'

Mr Ryder, a large, powerful-looking man, did not return the smile.

'What the devil's going on here?' he asked, and Mr Billings tried to answer, but his voice was drowned out by the dozen or so other people in reception all eager to voice their complaints. Mr Ryder held up his hands and waited for them to stop.

'All right,' he said, 'let's take this one at a time.' He pointed to the woman in the suit. 'You go first . . .'

★

Twenty minutes later, the computer fault was being repaired, the people having tea on the terrace had been moved indoors while the pond was being cleared, and the emergency exit to the car park had been opened so that guests could get their cars in and out. The only people left in the lobby, apart from Mr Ryder and Mr Billings, were Nicholas and Fiona.

'I'm sorry you've had to wait so long,' Mr Ryder said. 'What can I do for you both?'

'You don't have to worry about these two,' said Mr Billings. 'The boy is a troublemaker. I've already told him to leave.'

'I'm not a troublemaker,' said Nicholas. 'I'm here to ask why my mother –'

'Out!' shouted Mr Billings. 'I warned you. Get out, or I'll call the police.'

'Nobody is calling the police.' Mr Ryder's eyes narrowed as he looked at Nicholas. 'What's this about your mother?'

'I want to know,' said Nicholas, 'why she lost her job here when she was only doing what she was supposed to do.'

'This is ridiculous!' Mr Billings took a phone from his pocket. 'I'm calling for security to come and deal with him . . .'

Mr Ryder waved him to silence.

'What's your name?'

'Nicholas Frith.'

'I've heard of you.' Mr Ryder nodded slowly. 'Don't you go to school at Dent Valley?'

Nicholas admitted that he did.

'I have a friend who teaches there. Michael Daimon.' Mr Ryder paused. 'I am the owner of this hotel. If you have a complaint, perhaps you should talk to me.'

Mrs Frith got her job back. Mr Ryder actually called round to the house that evening in person to offer it to her. He said that Mr Billings and the girl on the desk had been dismissed. He had suspected them both of dishonesty for some time but been unable to prove anything and he was, he said, extremely grateful to Mrs Frith for the stand she had taken. He brought her an enormous bunch of flowers to apologize for the way she had been treated.

Mrs Frith invited him in for a drink, and the two of them passed a very pleasant couple of hours talking together. It turned out they had a good many common acquaintances in the hotel industry and had even worked together, albeit very briefly, one summer before Nicholas had been born. Mr Ryder said he would be taking over the management of the Royal himself for a while, and Mrs Frith assured him she would be very happy to come back and manage reception.

Mr Ryder did have one request, however. He said he had nothing against Nicholas personally, but he wondered if, in future, he would mind keeping away from the hotel. He did not know if there was any truth in the rumours he had heard, he admitted, but he would feel better if Nicholas promised never to come near it again.

In the circumstances, as Fiona later said, it seemed only fair to agree.

And after that, life really *was* rather good. It wasn't perfect, but it was vastly better than anything Nicholas might have expected.

Now that Miss Murajee had explained *why* the accidents happened, he was getting quite good at preventing them. By watching the people around him, he was often able to tell when they were becoming too agitated or emotional and, if they were, he would slip away quietly to a place where he could be alone, or to the Safe Room at school.

He still wasn't sure if Miss Murajee was right when she said that happiness was not something that happened to you but a decision, but he was changing his mind even on that. He watched Mr Gibbon one day, chuckling at the fact that he had squirted chocolate sauce on the fish fingers for supper instead of ketchup, and thought how easy it would have been for him to be upset and angry about it instead of amused. Mr Gibbon, after all, had more reason to be upset than most people but almost never was. In fact, he was the most consistently *happy* person that Nicholas had ever met.

Maybe, Nicholas thought, he shouldn't feel quite so sorry for himself about living under the curse, and should concentrate instead on enjoying the things he had – because the things he had were giving him a lot of pleasure. The accidents were almost under control. His mother was happier in her new job than he had seen her in years. His friend Fiona was proving to be cleverer and kinder every day than he could have believed and, on the odd occasions when things did go wrong, he had Miss Murajee and Mr Fender to turn to for help.

One way and another, he thought, life could be a lot worse. In fact, all things considered, he could hardly ask for it to get any better.

And then it did.

At breakfast one morning, his mother passed him a letter. It was from his father in America, asking if he would like to come out and visit him that summer.

CHAPTER NINE

Nicholas had never met his father. Dwight Dyer was an American from Cedar Falls in Iowa, who owned a company that made chewy toys for dogs. Twelve years ago, his business had brought him to England, where he found himself attracted to a young woman on the staff at his hotel – Rachel Frith. She, in turn, was rather taken with the tall, quiet American and, when he asked her out to the cinema, readily agreed.

The visit to the cinema was followed by a good many other trips out together and the two became very close. Close enough for Dwight to ask, when it was time to go back to America, if Rachel would come with him. There was, he admitted, the slight problem that he already had a fiancée back at home in Iowa, but he was going to tell her, on his return, that he had met someone else, and then Rachel could fly out and join him.

When Dwight got back to America, however, he found his fiancée, Mary-Beth, was expecting a baby. After many sleepless nights, much agonizing and a good many long and tearful phone calls to Rachel in England, he made his choice, and he and Mary-Beth were married in their church at Cedar Falls.

Two weeks later, Rachel Frith found that she was expecting a baby as well, and on Christmas Eve that year, Nicholas was born.

Mr Dyer behaved a lot better than some men do in this situation. He had made a bad mistake, but he did what he could to take responsibility for it. On the first day of every month, his lawyers sent a cheque to help cover the cost of bringing up his son and, every Christmas, he sent Nicholas a birthday card and two presents. With them, he would enclose a short letter, sending Nicholas his good wishes and enclosing a photograph. The photo usually showed Mr Dyer with his growing family (he had four children now) so that Nicholas could see what his half-brother and half-sisters looked like.

For the last two years, the presents had arrived broken – postmen had a tendency to fall over and drop things when they were delivering mail to the Frith household – but the photos were unharmed and Nicholas would often look at them, wondering what sort of a man his father was. The figure that stared back at him from the pictures had changed slightly over the years, putting on a little weight and losing a certain amount of hair, but the smile had stayed the same.

Most of the pictures also featured his half-brother, Zak, who was three months older than himself, and his three sisters, getting taller each year. Nicholas wondered what they were like as well, and whether he would ever see them, and whether he would like them if he did.

And now there was a letter. Two letters. One was from his father saying that, if his mother agreed, he would like to invite Nicholas to stay for three weeks in the summer holidays and meet the American side of his 'family'. He said he would be happy to cover any expenses, like the flight, and hoped that Nicholas would agree, as they all wanted very much to meet him.

The other letter was from his half-brother, Zak, and said much the same thing but in a less formal way. He said hi, and he really hoped Nicholas could come over as there was so much to do and life with three sisters was OK, but having a brother would be 'real neat'.

Another photo had come with Zak's letter, of his father surrounded by at least twenty other relations, and Nicholas wondered what it would be like to live with such a large family. In England, he had no grandparents, cousins or aunts. All his life it had been just him and his mother, and the more he looked at the picture, the more he wanted to go to America and see them all.

He wanted it a lot.

'If you're that keen,' said Fiona, 'then you should go.'

The children were sitting on a bench outside the science block at break. It was a wonderful sunny morning, showing the first touch of spring, and Fiona's eyes squinted in the light as she spoke.

'How can I?' Nicholas looked at her. 'I can't go anywhere under the curse, you know that.'

'I know it *used* to be true,' said Fiona, 'but it's not at the moment. Things hardly happen to you at all these days, do they?'

This was not entirely true. Only that morning, in tutor group, Miss Greco had found a couple of adders nestling under the radiator, but she had reacted very sensibly. She had moved the class to the library, while she called for someone to deal with the snakes, and there had been no real crisis. No one had been hurt.

But events like this were, Nicholas had noticed, getting fewer. In the last two weeks, he could remember only one serious incident at school, when a man giving a lecture on the power of the English longbow had inadvertently shot the history teacher, Mr Walker. Even then, he had not been badly hurt. The arrow made a couple of holes in his jacket when it pinned him to the wall, but the cut on his arm was little more than a graze.

Nicholas had learned what to do on those occasions when he felt the tension rising around him. He simply left the classroom and went to the Safe Room until Mr Fender or Fiona told him it was all right to come out. But if he went to America, there would be no Safe Room to go to. In Cedar Falls he would be putting his own family, some of them young children, at risk.

Fiona pointed out that at least they knew what the risk was. Nicholas had told his father, in one of his thank-you letters, about the trip to Spain and falling under the curse of Toribio de Cobrales.

'If you've told him about the curse,' said Fiona, 'and he still wants you to go, then you should go. He's said he doesn't mind.'

Nicholas was not so sure. It was one thing to say, from 3,000 miles away, that you didn't mind living with someone who attracted accidents and disasters, but it might be quite another when they actually started happening. And he did not want to cause any accidents around his father and his family. The last thing he wanted to do was hurt any of them and that was surely what would happen if he accepted the invitation. No, it was out of the question.

But he did take Fiona's advice on one thing. She said he should talk to Miss Murajee before he made a final decision, and he did.

Miss Murajee came in to school every Wednesday, to boost up the power in the Safe Room and to see how Nicholas was doing.

'I don't see why you shouldn't go,' she said, when he showed her the letter from his father. 'Wonderful country, America. Lovely people . . .'

'But what about the curse?'

'I think I agree with Fiona on that one.' Miss Murajee had set fire to a bunch of sage and was vigorously fanning the smoke around the room. 'You're managing the whole thing so much better these days. You've learnt how to keep the accident rate down. You should be all right.' She paused. 'The tricky bit's going to be the flying. On-board an aeroplane, with all those anxious emotions flooding the air and nowhere for you to go . . . But I might be able to help with that.'

'You might?' Nicholas felt his heart lifting.

'I could probably provide some sort of protection for the duration of the flight. And if you flew very early in the morning, while everyone's still a bit sleepy . . . yes, I think we could get you there safely. If you really wanted to go.'

It was exactly what Nicholas wanted to hear and he could not have been more pleased, although, as he pointed out to Miss Murajee, there was still one problem to overcome.

The letter from his father had said they would like him to come to America 'if his mother agreed', and Nicholas was not sure his mother would agree at all. He had a feeling she might think going to America was being disloyal in some way. Or that she might say he could go if he wanted, but make it clear she would be very upset if he did.

'You don't *know* that she'll be upset,' said Miss Murajee, 'and if she is, you can change your mind. But I think you should ask.'

So Nicholas did ask and, to his surprise, Mrs Frith not only agreed but thought it was an excellent idea.

'I was wondering what to do with you in August,' she said. 'I'm going to be standing in as Manager then, while Mr Ryder's in Scotland. I'll need to work all sorts of odd hours and I was wondering who to get to look after you.'

The final barrier was down, and Nicholas could hardly believe it. He had had very little to look forward to in the last year and a half, but now everything seemed to be coming together. He had found a friend, he had found a school that could cope with the curse, his mother had a job, the disasters were getting fewer every day – and he was going to America to see his father and meet his brother and sisters.

At the end of school that day, he walked back to Carlton Place with Fiona, in a mood of deep content. As they crossed the park, it began to rain, but he didn't mind. When they ran for shelter under the nearest tree, he even found he was laughing. Who cared about getting wet in a thunderstorm when you knew you were going to America?

At the tree, they found an elderly couple already sheltering under their umbrellas. The storm seemed to have blown up out of nowhere and taken most people by surprise. It was only four o'clock, but the sky was dark and tremendous thunderclaps rumbled through the air, following vivid flashes of lightning, while the rain came down in such torrents that it was impossible to see more than a few yards.

As they huddled together without even a coat, Nicholas glanced up to see the old couple looking down at him.

'Quite a storm, eh?' said the old man. 'Here.' He held out his umbrella. 'You take this. I'll share with the wife.'

'Thanks,' said Nicholas, and he was reaching out to take the offered umbrella, when the lightning struck.

Lightning travels at about 60,000 miles a second and a single bolt can deliver an electrical charge of anything up to a billion volts at a temperature of 50,000 degrees. This particular bolt hit the metal ferrule at the tip of the umbrella, travelled down its steel shaft and entered the old man. Electricity always seeks the shortest way of getting to ground, so it travelled down his arm, through his body, and into the earth beneath.

The smile was still frozen on the old man's face as he fell, and the deafening blast of thunder was still rolling around the park as he landed, face down on the grass, and lay there, the rain splashing on to his back. There was smoke coming from the bottom of his boots. Real smoke, rising into the air in little wisps.

The wind caught at the umbrella he had been offering to Nicholas and blew it from his grasp. It bowled excitedly away across the park and for a moment Nicholas wondered if he should run after it and fetch it.

'What happened?' The old woman was staring

down at her husband. 'Did he trip over something? Is he all right?'

'Call an ambulance,' said Fiona as she knelt down and gently rolled the man on to his back before loosening his shirt and tie. She listened to his chest for a moment then pulled open his mouth, put his head back, pinched his nose and carefully breathed into his lungs. While Nicholas dialled 999 on his mobile, the old woman was still asking what had happened.

'I don't understand,' she kept saying. 'I was looking the other way. What happened to him?'

Fiona did not answer. She concentrated instead on blowing air into the old man's lungs. Blow . . . check the rise of his chest . . . watch it fall again . . . wait . . . blow again. That was what they had taught her to do in the St John Ambulance class and they had told her you should keep doing it until someone more qualified told you to stop. So that's what she did.

The ambulance arrived very quickly. It came careering towards them over the sodden grass with the paramedics jumping out before it had even come to a halt, but both Nicholas and Fiona already knew it was no good.

The old man – neither of them even knew his name – was dead.

CHAPTER TEN

'Thank you so much for coming.' Mrs Frith ushered Miss Murajee into the hall. 'We didn't know who else to call, and I've been so worried.'

'Where is he?' asked Miss Murajee.

'He's upstairs. He came in after . . . after it happened, went up to bed and he's been there ever since.'

Fiona was standing at the bottom of the stairs, looking rather solemn. 'He won't talk to us or anything,' she said.

'He won't talk, he won't eat . . .' Mrs Frith was clearly worried. 'All he does is lie there.'

'Right . . .' Miss Murajee nodded. 'I'll see what I can do.'

She went upstairs to Nicholas's room. The

curtains were drawn, but in the dim light she could see him lying on the bed, his face to the wall. He did not move or speak as she came in.

'Nicholas?' Miss Murajee walked over to the bed. 'What is this? What's going on?'

There was no answer.

'Nicholas!' Her voice was firm and commanding. 'You have to talk to me.'

'There's nothing to talk about,' said Nicholas eventually. 'I killed him, didn't I?'

'The old man in the park? Is that what this is about?'

'It's bad enough when people around me get injured, but when they start dying . . .'

'The way I heard it,' said Miss Murajee, 'is that a man in the park was struck by lightning, and that you and Fiona did everything you could to help. You called for an ambulance, she did first aid, and his wife was very grateful.'

'She doesn't know, though, does she?' said Nicholas. 'She doesn't know it was my fault.'

'And you do?' Miss Murajee sat on the edge of the bed. 'How do you know it wasn't a coincidence? That it wouldn't have happened anyway?'

'I'm a lightning conductor,' said Nicholas. 'You told me that yourself.'

'Oh, come on! I didn't mean it literally! Plenty

of people get hit by lightning. Are you the cause of it every time? Of course you're not.'

Nicholas refused to be consoled. He had thought that his life was getting back to normal, and he had been wrong. His life could never be normal. He had been a fool ever to think it could. A fool to think he could live like other children. A fool to think he could go to America and meet his father . . .

His face still turned to the wall, a tear trickled down his cheek.

'Bad things happen to people,' said Miss Murajee softly. 'They happen to all of us. It doesn't mean it's your fault.'

'So whose fault is it?' asked Nicholas. 'People around me get hurt. Yesterday it was an old man in the park – who's next? Fiona? My mum? You?' He took a deep breath. 'It has to stop. It can't go on like this. It has to stop.'

'Ah . . .' Miss Murajee nodded. 'So that's the plan. You're going to lie here in the dark until you die, is that it? You think that's going to help?'

'It has to stop,' Nicholas repeated doggedly. 'If I go anywhere it means someone gets hurt.'

There was a pause before Miss Murajee spoke again.

'You asked me once if I could do anything to lift the curse. Well, I can't, but I've been doing some reading, talking to a few friends and . . . it seems there might be a way.'

Nicholas rolled on to his back and looked at her for the first time.

'A way to lift the curse?'

'Possibly.'

'You can get rid of it? Completely?'

'*I* can't,' said Miss Murajee. 'I told you. It's beyond my strength to remove. But it seems there is one person who might be able to resist it, despite its power.'

'Who?'

'You,' said Miss Murajee. 'It's you.' She stood up. 'Come and see me when you're feeling better and we'll talk about it.'

The doctor had said that Nicholas should take as much time as he needed to recover from the shock of the events in the park, so the next morning, instead of going to school, he went round to Miss Murajee's house and knocked on the door.

She led him through the hallway of the little terraced house into a tiny walled garden at the back. The ground was covered with flowers and strangely scented herbs in dozens of pots and baskets and stone troughs. There were more plants growing in boxes on the brick walls all round, and Miss Murajee picked her way through the greenery to a table with two chairs before motioning Nicholas to sit down.

'I'll warn you now,' she said, 'it's not going to be easy. What I'm going to ask you to do will seem strange and you'll need to be very determined to do it. You'll wonder soon why you started it, but you'll have to promise to go on with it anyway and stick with it till it's finished. Can you do that?'

Nicholas said that he could. He was a little unnerved by the serious look on Miss Murajee's face but, if there was any chance of getting rid of Toribio's curse, he was determined to take it, whatever the cost.

'What do I have to do?' he asked.

Miss Murajee did not answer directly. Instead, she said, 'Do you know what magic is?'

It was not something Nicholas had ever really thought about, but he presumed it was about learning spells, waving wands and making potions from strange ingredients.

'No, no.' Miss Murajee waved a hand dismissively. 'Those things help, of course, but they are not the magic. What magic is . . .' She stopped and looked carefully at Nicholas. 'What magic really is, is *believing*. That's what the old wizards and sorcerers used to do, they *believed* things. They used spells and magic signs and all the other tricks to *help* them believe things, but the power came from the believing.'

'What Toribio de Cobrales did was set up a belief that anyone who disturbed his grave would be cursed, and it was such a strong belief that even three hundred years later it was still there. When you came along, it was strong enough to make you believe it. And once you believed it, you made it come true.'

'*I* made it come true?'

'That's how the magic works. What we believe becomes the truth, and what you have to do now is believe that you're not unlucky.'

'But I *am* unlucky,' said Nicholas.

'You've been made to *believe* that you are,' Miss Murajee corrected him patiently. 'And, as I said, we have to change that belief.'

'So what did she tell you to do?' asked Fiona.

Sitting with his friend in the classroom the following morning, Nicholas hesitated before answering. What Miss Murajee had told him to do was not what he had expected at all.

When she had warned him that the work of lifting the spell would be difficult and require every ounce of his determination, he had imagined that it might involve eating weird potions, performing strange rituals or battling unknown demons in a different dimension. But Miss Murajee had not asked him to do anything like that.

What she had done, was give him five sentences to repeat. He had to say them ten times in the morning when he woke up, ten times in the evening before he went to bed, and once every hour, on the hour, in between.

'Sentences?' asked Fiona. 'You mean some sort of spell?'

Nicholas didn't think they were a spell. They were just . . . sentences. The first one was: *I am very lucky and good things happen to me all the time.*

'But you're not lucky,' said Fiona. 'That's the whole problem, isn't it?'

'I know,' said Nicholas. 'But she says that saying it will make me think I am.'

'Ah . . .' Fiona nodded doubtfully. 'What are the others?'

The other sentences were:

I help the people around me, and good things happen to them all the time.
I like all animals and birds, and they like me.
I love gardening and enjoy working with plants.
I am happy, because I know that whatever happens is all right.

'And Miss Murajee thinks,' said Fiona, 'that if you say them often enough, you'll start to believe them?'

Nicholas nodded.

'And will that make any difference?' Fiona hesitated. 'I mean, even if you believe them, they still won't actually be true . . . will they?'

Nicholas was not sure. He had not entirely followed Miss Murajee's argument on this, though he did remember that, while she was talking, she had been very convincing.

Whether he understood or not, however, he was definitely decided on one thing. He was going to give it a try. After the incident in the park, something had to change, and this looked like his only chance. If there were even the remotest possibility of its working, he would do it. For as long as it took.

He had the sentences written out on a large card and, first thing every morning, he would get out of bed and sit at his desk and read them out loud, ten times. He had a smaller card with the sentences written on that he carried around with him during the day and every hour, on the hour, he would take it out and read them quietly to himself. In the evening, last thing before he went to bed, he would stand in front of his desk again. This time, before he read the sentences, he would take a sprig of dried herbs that Miss Murajee had given him, light the end with a match and, as the smoke rose to the ceiling, read the sentences aloud.

It might sound simple enough, but Miss Murajee was right when she had warned him it would not be easy. Nicholas found it very difficult to remember to read the sentences at the right time during the day. A lot of times he forgot, and Miss Murajee told him not to worry but to say them when he remembered and try not to forget in future. But he still did. In the end, he bought himself a watch with an alarm that vibrated on his wrist so that he knew it was time – and would take out his card and read it.

I am very lucky, and good things happen to me all the time . . .

Very soon, he knew all the sentences by heart, but he still carried around the card and took it out and read them.

I help the people around me, and good things happen to them all the time . . .

The only trouble was that good things *didn't* happen to the people around him all the time. Sometimes, the things that happened to them were very bad. Like the time Miss Bingley got zapped by a robot in her textiles lesson.

The robot had been built by a talented Year 11

student as his GCSE design tech project, and was programmed to herd sheep. Miss Bingley was a quiet, gentle woman, who was trying to teach 7E how to knit a scarf when, activated by the sound of her voice, the robot unexpectedly came to life and began herding everyone to the far end of the room. It had been fitted, as Miss Bingley sadly discovered, with a cattle prod capable of delivering several hundred volts to any animal that tried to resist it, and in no time the entire class was huddled in a corner of the room with the robot in front of them, wagging its electronic tail.

They might have been there most of the day if Miss Bingley had not managed to press the panic button on her desk before the robot took her down. In a matter of minutes, Mr Fender had arrived. He took in the situation at a glance, picked up a crow bar from one of the work benches and swiftly disabled the machine.

Although no one had been seriously hurt, Miss Bingley was visibly shaken – she was still twitching a week later – and several of the children were badly upset. How could he keep saying to himself that good things happened all the time, Nicholas thought, when the opposite was so obviously true? How was he ever going to make himself believe he was helping the people around him when anyone could see that what he was actually doing was making life very difficult for them?

He tried to explain his feelings to Miss Murajee, on her visit to the school the next Wednesday, but she didn't seem to think there was anything to worry about.

'Sounds to me like some very good things happened,' she said, placing a fresh sprig of herbs in the vase on the table in the Safe Room. 'The headmaster's alarm system worked brilliantly, the problem was sorted before anyone was hurt . . .' She looked at Nicholas. 'What's wrong with any of that?'

'You know what's wrong. It wouldn't have happened if I hadn't been there, and people do get hurt. They get hurt all the time.'

Only that morning, a boy in Nicholas's class had been attacked by a woodpecker trying to drill a hole in his knee. It was not easy to say '*good things happen to the people around me*' with any conviction, with that sort of thing going on.

'I've told you,' said Miss Murajee, 'you don't have to *believe* it. You just have to say it.'

'But I don't see how it's going to help,' protested Nicholas. 'I mean, even if I did believe it, it's still not going to be true, is it? What's the point of believing something that's not true?'

'If you believe it,' said Miss Murajee, 'then it will be true. That's how the magic works. When you believe something, you make it happen.'

'Are you sure?' Nicholas looked at her doubtfully. 'Most people think it's the other way round.'

'And most people are wrong,' said Miss Murajee firmly. She took his head between her hands and her eyes bored down at his. 'What you are doing has more power than you can possibly imagine. The change is already happening and I promise you, I *promise* you that this will work. And you will be free.'

As she spoke, Nicholas could feel determination and confidence flooding through his body. He believed her. If he did what Miss Murajee said, if he followed her advice, if he repeated the sentences every hour as she had instructed, the curse would be lifted and all would be well. He knew it was true!

So he went home and he did it.

He did it every morning, every evening and every hour, day after day and week after week.

And it still didn't work.

CHAPTER ELEVEN

There were times when Nicholas thought it was getting better. In those first few days and weeks, as he said the sentences to himself, there were several occasions when he was convinced that the spell had been broken and that he was no longer unlucky. But then he would pick a leaf from a tree and watch it blacken and wither in his fingers, or he would walk towards a dog on the pavement and watch it snarl and back away in fear, and realize nothing had changed at all.

On one occasion, convinced that the power of Toribio's spell had, at the very least, weakened dramatically, he tried to take a test. It was a history test given by Miss MacMahon to see how much the class remembered about the wives of

Henry VIII. There were only ten questions and, as she read out the first of them, Nicholas reached secretly for a bit of scrap paper. But the instant he started writing, Miss MacMahon began one of her nosebleeds, pints of blood spurted on to her desk and the floor, and the class had to be abandoned.

The accidents continued, much as always. The ones at school were not too serious these days, with the Safe Room and Mr Fender's alarm system, but at home, for a while, they actually got worse.

The woman in the house next door had moved away – people who lived near Nicholas often discovered they would rather live somewhere else – and a new neighbour had arrived, called Mr Runciman. He was a short man, with short bristly hair, and an even shorter temper. In the three weeks that he lived next door, he tripped over carpets, fell down stairs, trapped his fingers in doors, burnt himself on ovens, gave himself electric shocks and got a pound coin stuck up his nose. In the end, he went to live with his sister in Scotland, and whenever Nicholas thought of him, he felt rather depressed.

He told Miss Murajee that he didn't think her plan was working, but she said he needed to be patient. He asked how long he should be patient for, and she said she had no idea. It might be weeks. It could be years. It was not very encouraging and, as time went on, Nicholas found it more and more difficult to imagine that things would ever change. He would never be able to believe the way Miss Murajee said he had to believe and he knew, deep down, that he was always going to be the unluckiest boy in the world.

But for some reason, despite all this, he carried on saying the sentences. He said them standing in front of his desk every morning when he woke up: *I am very lucky and good things happen to me all the time . . .*

He said them again in the evening before he went to bed: *I help the people around me, and good things happen to them all the time . . .*

And he said them every hour during the day. By now, he no longer needed the watch with the vibrating alarm. Some clock in his brain would tell him the time and he would start reciting: *I like all animals and birds, and they like me . . .*

He had said the words so often that he no longer even listened while he was saying them. *I love gardening and enjoy working with plants . . .* It was like doing it in his sleep. In fact, one night, he found he was doing exactly that. It was three o'clock in the morning and he woke up to find himself reciting: *I am always happy, because I know that whatever happens is all right . . .*

If you had asked him why he was doing it, he would not have been able to tell you. He no longer believed it would work, but saying the sentences had become part of his life. Like getting dressed or cleaning his teeth, it was just something he did. Every morning, every evening, and every hour through the day.

Two weeks before the end of term, Mr Daimon came back.

The science teacher had been away for nearly two months and returned a changed man. The loud voice, the brusque manner and the barely concealed irritation had gone. He was relaxed, calm and spoke in a quiet, gentle voice. He had, he told Nicholas, been on a course of intensive psychotherapy with an emphasis on anger management.

'Something I should have done years ago,' he said. 'It did me a power of good, getting rid of all those feelings about my father . . .' For a moment, his fists clenched spasmodically, but he took a deep breath and relaxed again.

'I wanted to thank you. The headmaster told me about your . . . your problem, and how the accidents happened. It must be very difficult for you, but I want you to know it worked out well for me. Best thing that could have happened, really. Made me sort myself out. Odd, isn't it!'

Nicholas agreed that it was.

'And of course I'm not the only one you've helped, am I? We've all seen what you've done for Fiona. What a change, eh?'

Nicholas was not aware that he had done anything for Fiona, but he did know that she was a very different girl from the one with the bad haircut and the ill-fitting clothes that he had first seen that day in Mr Fender's office.

'Hardly recognized her when she walked into the lab,' said Mr Daimon. 'I thought she was someone new! And as for the schoolwork . . . !'

Fiona's schoolwork had improved dramatically. She had enjoyed coming top in the French test she had worked for with Nicholas. In fact, she had liked it so much that she decided to repeat the experience. She worked hard for the next test, and came top again. The next week, she tried the same technique in maths, with a similar result, and then in science. In the last month, in all three subjects, her work had put her with the top two or three in the class.

'She's a lot cleverer than any of us realized, and I'm not sure she'd have found that out without you.' Mr Daimon smiled cheerily at Nicholas. 'It's good to know something positive has come out of it all, isn't it?'

Nicholas agreed that it was. And he knew he should be grateful for all the changes that had happened in his life since the start of term. He had Fiona as the best of possible friends. Miss Murajee and Mr Fender had found a way to let him live in a manner that was very close to normal. Mr Gibbon was teaching him the piano. His mother was happier than he had seen her in years and yet . . . and yet . . .

Nothing could alter the fact that he was still living under the curse. The prison might be more comfortable, it might even have brought the occasional benefit, but it was still a prison.

The days passed, and the weeks, and the months. Term ended, the Easter holidays came, the summer term began . . . and Nicholas discovered a new hobby. He took up gardening.

It started in the Easter holidays when Fiona and Mr Gibbon went to Yorkshire for a week to stay with Mr Gibbon's sister. His mother was at work, Nicholas was spending large parts of the day on his own, and it left him with a lot of time on his hands and nothing really to do.

Miss Murajee had been supplying all the herbs

she used for the Safe Room and for Nicholas to keep on his desk from her own tiny backyard, and was finding it difficult to provide a sufficient quantity. Nicholas, on the other hand, had a large garden at the back of his house. It was big enough for him and Fiona to kick a football around at weekends and Miss Murajee suggested that he use part of it to grow some of the herbs he needed for himself.

She gave him cuttings and showed him how to make them root in pots and then how to clear a patch of ground where he could plant them out. It was a peaceful occupation, safely away from other people, and Nicholas found he enjoyed it. During the week that Fiona was on holiday, he not only planted the herbs, but set about clearing a fruit cage containing some very healthy raspberry canes, and then planted a flower bed.

He worked wearing gloves and found being out in the open air, tending the plants, and watching them grow, deeply satisfying. When Fiona came back, he continued to find time at weekends and in the evenings to keep his garden going. He had, his mother said, a real knack for it.

And he was out in the garden one day early in June, planting out some hollyhocks that he had grown from seed, when a voice said, 'Who are you?'

Looking up, Nicholas saw a boy, about four years old, leaning over the fence from the next-door garden. Small children always made him nervous. They could have accidents before you could blink.

'I'm Nicholas,' he said. 'Be careful you don't fall down.'

'I live here now.' The boy pointed to the house which had, until recently, belonged to the short-tempered Mr Runciman. Nicholas vaguely remembered hearing that it had been sold.

'I'm Brian.' The boy looked around the garden with an admiring gaze. 'Is all this yours?'

'Yes,' said Nicholas.

The boy took in the fruit cage with the raspberries, the brightly coloured flowers and the lawn with the football goal.

'You're lucky,' he said.

Three months before, if someone had told Nicholas he was lucky, he would instantly have rejected the idea. After all, he was not lucky. He was the unluckiest boy in the world. But our thoughts are governed, as much as anything, by habit. Most of them are simple repetitions of ideas we have had a thousand times before and they flash along well-worn paths in our brains so fast that we barely notice them.

Three months before, the most familiar path

for Nicholas's thoughts would have been the belief that he was unlucky, but this time, they found a different route. There was an easier and wider track for them to follow. It was one that had been built into his brain over the days and weeks of endless repetition. Those thousands of times he had said the same thing over and over again had created a path as wide and inviting as an empty motorway, and his thoughts followed this new route as inevitably as the river finds its bed.

The boy said, 'You're lucky,' and the thought that instantly sprang into Nicholas's head was that he was right. He *was* lucky. And good things happened to him all the time. Just for one instant, before he was even aware that he was thinking it, the thought was in his mind, unquestioned and accepted. Just for one instant, he believed it.

And in that instant of belief, the world changed.

For a moment, it changed quite literally. With his eyes still open, Nicholas found he was no longer standing in the garden, but in a large room with stone walls supporting a great beamed roof, and a flagged floor beneath his feet. The room was completely empty except for a man at the far end, sitting at a table in front of an enormous fire.

He was dressed in a black tunic over baggy

trousers that stopped just below the knee. On his head he wore a wide-brimmed hat, round his neck hung a green stone on a silver chain, and from his chin flowed a long grey beard. He seemed quite unaware of Nicholas as he busily scratched at a piece of a parchment with a pen made from a goose feather.

As he wrote, little flashes of light appeared from his body, and danced and floated in the air around him. After a moment, one of the lights started moving towards Nicholas.

It moved with gathering speed and, as it flew through the air, became an arrow, pointing straight at his head. There was another light following it, and that one became an axe, and the one after it became a knife. They raced towards him, but before they reached him, they stopped as if they had bumped into some invisible barrier, turned back into a shower of lights, and disappeared.

Other lights were still leaving the old man and became more weapons. They turned into stones that fell from the ceiling, flaming torches and evil-looking demons that danced across the floor, but Nicholas always knew that he was perfectly safe. None of them could reach him through the shield that protected him.

Then, watching the display, it occurred to him

that he would be safe even without the shield. After all, though the rocks and arrows that flew towards him might look dangerous, they were not real. They were only made of light. Even if he were to step out from behind the shield, he would come to no harm.

And so he did. He stepped carefully to one side, and watched as an iron hammer hurled itself at his chest. It passed straight through him, with no more power to hurt or harm than a gun fired on the screen in the cinema. It was the same with all the other weapons that hurled themselves at his body. As long as you knew they weren't real, they couldn't hurt you.

On the other side of the room, the old man still seemed quite unaware of his presence, and Nicholas felt a surge of anger. The stones and arrows might not be real but they had been frightening enough before he knew that. What gave this man the right to go about scaring other people? On the wall beside him hung a collection of spears. He took down one of them, and held it for a moment before reaching back his arm and flinging it with all his strength towards the old man.

It landed, point first, on the table, right in the middle of the piece of parchment. The old man looked up in surprise, peered at it for a moment and then turned to look at Nicholas.

His eyes were very dark and, under his gaze, Nicholas was aware of a great power. For a long minute, the two of them stared at each other and then . . . and then the old man smiled. It was the barest flicker of a smile and it touched only the corner of his lips, but it was there and Nicholas saw it. At the same time, he gave the faintest nod of his head, as if Nicholas had made a request and he had agreed to it. Then he calmly turned back to his desk, picked up his goose-feather quill and continued writing.

An instant later both he and the room had gone.

Back in the garden, everything looked just the same. Nicholas was standing by the flower bed with his tray of hollyhocks and Brian, the little boy next door, was peering at him from over the fence . . . but nothing was the same really. Everything had changed. Nicholas could feel it in every cell of his body.

A cat strolled calmly across the lawn towards him, briefly brushing past his leg before moving on. He took off a glove, reached down and picked one of the hollyhock seedlings. It lay in his hand, bright and clear and green.

There was no doubt.

The spell had been broken, and he was free.

CHAPTER TWELVE

When Fiona came back from her St John Ambulance class, she found Nicholas waiting for her outside the flat in Carlton Place. He was looking a little dazed and she thought at first that something bad must have happened to him.

'Are you all right?' she asked.

'I think so.' Nicholas held out a bunch of flowers. 'I came to give you these.'

They were snapdragons he had grown in his garden, and it was only as Fiona reached out to take them that she noticed he wasn't wearing any gloves.

She gave a little gasp. 'What . . . what's happened?'

'Well.' Nicholas took a deep breath. 'I think it's worked.'

As he told her what had happened earlier that morning, Fiona, normally so calm, let out so many shrieks and screams of excitement that Mr Gibbon opened the window to ask what all the noise was about.

'It's Nicholas,' Fiona told him. 'He's not unlucky any more!'

Mr Gibbon had always found it difficult to believe that Nicholas lived under a curse. As far as he was concerned Nicholas had been nothing but good news from the first day Fiona brought him home, but he didn't want to appear rude. If Nicholas was happy, then good luck to the lad.

'I think that calls for a celebration,' he said. 'Let's all have a chocolate biscuit. No, hang the expense. It's a big day, let's have two.'

Mrs Frith, on the desk in the Royal Hotel, took a little more convincing. Nicholas and Fiona walked round there from Carlton Place and, even when she had seen Nicholas take a flower from one of the displays, and happily stroke a dog that was crossing the reception hall, she still found it difficult to believe.

She was worried that he might have imagined it all, and she was even more worried when a man rang from the sixth floor saying he was going to jump out of the window if someone didn't bring him a decent-sized bar of soap. But Nicholas never doubted the truth of what had happened.

'It's no good looking like that,' he said firmly. 'It's nothing to do with me.'

On Monday morning, Mr Fender was waiting at the school gates to ask if the rumours he had heard were true and, when Nicholas said that they were, the headmaster swept him straight off to his office to hear the full story.

'Extraordinary,' he murmured to himself as Nicholas repeated the details of what had happened in the garden on Saturday morning. 'And you're quite sure, are you? The curse has definitely gone?'

'Definitely,' said Nicholas. 'I've been doing all the things it said I couldn't, and there haven't been any accidents. The only thing I haven't done yet is take a test.'

'Well . . .' Mr Fender picked up his pen. 'That should be easy enough to arrange.' He would have liked to call Miss Murajee first to check that there was no risk, but she was away in Ireland doing a course on Seeing into the Future.

'I'll tell the staff, and one of them can give you a test some time this morning. Then we'll know for certain, eh?'

In the staffroom at break that morning, when

Mr Fender asked if any of his teachers would like to give Nicholas a test as a final demonstration that all was well, his request was met with a distinct lack of enthusiasm. Everyone remembered all too clearly what had happened before.

In the end, it was Mr Daimon who stepped forward and offered to give his class a short test on thermodynamics. He said Nicholas had done more than anyone to help turn his life around and that, in the circumstances, it was the least he could do.

While the test was going on, Mr Fender hovered outside in the corridor, occasionally peering in through the window of the science room to check that everything was all right. He rather admired the way that Mr Daimon constantly reassured the class that it was perfectly safe and there was nothing to worry about, and only someone very close would have seen the slight beads of perspiration on his forehead.

Nicholas did the test, and nothing happened. It might be hard to believe that doing a test in school could make you happy, but Nicholas could not have been more pleased. It was the last sign that his life was completely back to normal, and the delight shone in his face.

Mr Fender came in at the end of the lesson

and Nicholas showed him the finished paper. The headmaster looked down the answers, nodding with satisfaction.

'Excellent,' he said. 'All we need to do now is teach you to get some of them right.'

Unlike Mrs Frith, Miss Murajee needed no proof that the curse had been lifted. She took one look at Nicholas standing on her doorstep and her face broadened into a huge smile.

'Well, well, well!' she boomed, as she ushered him inside. 'Congratulations! When did it happen?' She led him through to the kitchen, sat him down and listened with the greatest interest to his story.

'That was Toribio all right,' she said as Nicholas described the man at the table with the green stone round his neck. 'Or a part of him at least.'

'But I thought he was dead?'

'Only his body. The rest of him sounds healthy enough.'

Nicholas had brought some raspberries from his garden as a thank-you present, and Miss Murajee spooned them into a couple of bowls and poured cream over the top.

'I have to tell you I'm impressed. That was a powerful piece of magic. Not easy to throw off at all. You did well!'

'Thank you,' said Nicholas. 'There was a question I wanted to ask, if that's all right?'

'Fire ahead,' Miss Murajee picked up a spoon.

Nicholas hesitated. The question he wanted to ask was something he had been thinking about, on and off, ever since he had broken free from the curse, but he wasn't entirely sure how to phrase it.

'I know,' he said, eventually, 'that telling myself I was lucky all those hundreds of times meant that I broke the spell, but does it mean that I really am going to be lucky from now on? Am I going to be as lucky as I was unlucky, or will I just go back to being like I was before?'

'Ah,' Miss Murajee said, smiling at him over the top of her glasses, 'that depends. Do you believe you're going to be lucky?'

'I don't know,' said Nicholas. 'That's why I was asking you.'

'Well.' Miss Murajee was still smiling. 'Like I said . . . it depends.'

Mrs Frith decided to have a party.

'We need to say thank you,' she told Nicholas, 'to all the people who helped us get through this. We'd never have done it without them.'

The date she chose was the first Saturday after the end of term, and Fiona and Mr Gibbon came over in the morning to help get everything ready. The weather that day was so warm that Mrs Frith decided to move everything out of doors, and the children helped her carry the dining table out into the garden to a patch of shade under a large ash tree.

Mr Gibbon helped Mrs Frith prepare the food in the kitchen, while Fiona and Nicholas spent the day making decorations, hanging lanterns and coloured lights among the trees, blowing up balloons and setting out the chairs.

At six o'clock, the first guests to arrive were Mr Fender and Mr Daimon, who brought with them a dozen bottles of champagne in a tin bath full of ice. They were carrying it round to the back of the house as Mr Ryder appeared with a huge box of fireworks, accompanied by Miss Murajee, dressed in a bright red sari with gold edging. She gave Nicholas a small silver disc with symbols etched on both sides that she said might be useful as a charm when he went to see his father in America.

Free of the curse, Nicholas had accepted the invitation to spend part of his summer holiday in Cedar Falls and was flying to Des Moines in Iowa in four days' time. It was a prospect that made him very excited, if a little nervous.

'No need to be nervous,' said Miss Murajee,

her eyes twinkling. 'I've been looking into my crystal ball, and it all goes brilliantly. You have a wonderful time there. In fact you both do. You and Fiona.'

'But I'm not going with Fiona,' said Nicholas. 'I'm going on my own.'

Miss Murajee looked puzzled for a moment, but then her face cleared.

'Quite right. So you are. It's *next* year you go together, isn't it. Your mother takes over as manager of the Royal, Mr Gibbon gets a job there playing the piano, and you two go off to America.' She gave a throaty chuckle. 'My goodness, but you have some adventures, I can tell you!'

Nicholas would have liked to ask her what the adventures were, but at that moment the last of the guests arrived. It was Señor Herez, the man who had helped save Nicholas's life in Spain nearly two years before.

Señor Herez had heard from Mrs Frith that Nicholas had broken free from the curse and had written to say he was coming to England in two weeks' time on business, and could he call in to congratulate them in person. He had driven down from Heathrow that afternoon and brought with him not only his grandmother, Donna Alena, looking smaller and frailer than ever, but Miguel, the man who had driven the taxi on that fateful journey into the mountains. He said he hoped Mrs Frith wouldn't mind the extra visitors, but both of them had wanted to see Nicholas and hear his story for themselves.

Miguel produced a bag of presents he had brought from the farmhouse in Spain – rounds of cheese, a leg of ham, some figs and a bottle of apricot brandy – and Donna Alena produced a photograph of the grave of Toribio, which she wanted to show Nicholas. With Señor Herez translating her words into English, she explained that the grave had been repaired and was now surrounded, as he could see, by a metal fence and a warning sign in seven languages advising people to stay away.

'Since you left,' Señor Herez explained, 'we have tried to make sure that the same thing does not happen to anyone else.'

It was a magical party. Whether it was Mr Ryder's champagne, or the food, or simply the unexpected warmth of an English summer evening, Nicholas never knew, but it was one of those special times that people remember for years afterwards and can't help smiling about when they do.

The food was wonderful. There were great rounds of home-made pizza, slices of cold meats, barbecued sausages, curried chicken, loaves of warm garlic bread, pastries, sauces and bowls of a dozen different sorts of salad. While they ate, Mr Ryder kept pouring the champagne and they sat round the table under the ash tree in the light of the setting sun, and talked.

Most of the talk was about Nicholas and how he had managed to break free from the spell. It was a long story, and with everyone describing their own part in it, and Señor Herez translating everything into Spanish for his grandmother and Miguel to understand, it took even longer to tell. But nobody seemed to mind. It was, they all agreed, a most astonishing tale, and they might still have been discussing it at midnight if Nicholas had not reminded his mother that there were puddings indoors and if she wanted anyone to eat them it might be a good idea to bring them out.

The sun was going down and, while the children cleared the table and Mr Fender lit the candles on sticks that were supposed to keep away the midges and mosquitoes, Mr Ryder went down to the bottom of the garden and set off a thunderous volley of rockets that showered golden sparks all over the night sky. Then everyone helped themselves to slices of gateau and tart and bowls of fruit salad and cream that Mrs Frith had provided and, when they had eaten far more than was good for them, they sat back in their chairs and listened to Mr Gibbon, who was indoors playing the piano.

It was a perfect summer's night. The air was still and warm, and the sky was a deep velvet blue in which the stars shone with an astonishing clarity. The Milky Way blazed in the great arc that spanned a hundred thousand light years and on either side the constellations wheeled their stately dance round the pole star. Sitting back in his chair and staring up into the night, Nicholas thought he had never felt happier in his life.

Around him, the air was filled with the quiet murmur of conversation. Señor Herez and Mr Ryder were deep in a discussion about olive farming; Donna Alena and Miss Murajee were discussing magic in Latin, the only language they had in common; and Mr Daimon was telling Mrs Frith about the problems he had had with his father. Indoors, Mr Gibbon could still be heard playing softly on the piano, and Fiona was looking after Miguel who had got cramp in his right calf muscle. *Straighten knee, flex foot to stretch calf muscle, massage affected area.*

Nicholas watched her admiringly. It didn't matter if it was a scratch or a major injury, Fiona always knew how to deal with it. He remembered that first morning when she had dealt with

Mr Daimon's head wound after he had fallen down the stairs and thought, not for the first time, how lucky he was to have found her as a friend.

And it wasn't just Fiona. Every one of the people around him had helped him in some way through the events of the last two years. Every one of them had offered support at a time when it would have been much safer simply to walk away. If Miguel had not driven off to get help in the taxi that day in the mountains, or if Señor Herez had not been willing to come out when he was asked, or there had been no Donna Alena to weave her protective spell, he might not be alive today. And what would have happened to him if Mr Fender had not decided to make the changes in his school that meant Nicholas could stay? Or if he had not gone to the trouble of tracking down Miss Murajee? Looking round the table, he could not help thinking he had been very lucky.

Yes. That was it. Lucky . . .

In a way, you could say he had been lucky right from the start. Lucky on the mountainside in Spain to have found people who knew what to do to help. Lucky in England to have found a friend like Fiona, or a woman as clever as Miss Murajee. He had been lucky to find all these people who had wanted to help, or known how to help, or who had stood by him whether they could help or not . . .

He looked up, suddenly aware that everyone else at the table was looking at him expectantly. As if someone had asked him a question and the others were all waiting for him to answer.

'Nicholas!' Fiona was tugging at his sleeve. 'She's talking to you!'

'Who?'

'I was saying,' said Miss Murajee, 'that, yes, you are right. And that I think you have answered your question.'

'But the rest of us don't know what she's talking about,' said Fiona, 'because we don't know what you were thinking.'

Nicholas looked round the table. At his mother, looking at him a little anxiously in case something was wrong. At big, gruff Mr Ryder. At Mr Fender, who had drunk rather a lot of champagne and quietly fallen asleep. At Mr Daimon, looking remarkably relaxed and jolly. At Mr Gibbon, still indoors, his fingers splashing gently over the keyboard. At the three Spaniards, who had travelled hundreds of miles just to congratulate him. At Miss Murajee. And at Fiona, sitting beside him, waiting for an answer.

'It wasn't anything really,' he said. 'I was just thinking how lucky I was.'

And he has been lucky from that day to this.

ANDREW NORRISS

THE TOUCHSTONE

The Touchstone has all the answers.
The trick is knowing the right question.

puffin.co.uk

If you had a million pounds,
how would you spend it?

Whatever you were thinking,
read *Matt's Million* and think again.

ANDREW NORRISS

Matt's Million

SCHOOL

ANDREW NORRISS

AQUILA

Where does IT come from?

What does IT do?

IT's a spaceship from the past –
but can IT change the future?

Winner of the Whitbread Children's Book Award
and Silver Smarties Prize

puffin.co.uk